Lewis

THE MCCADE DRAGON BOOK 5

KATHI S. BARTON

This is a work of fiction. Names, characters, places, and incidents are products of the author's imagination or are used fictitiously and are not to be construed as real. Any resemblance to actual events, locations, organizations, or persons, living or dead, is entirely coincidental.

World Castle Publishing, LLC
Pensacola, Florida

Copyright © Kathi S. Barton 2018
Paperback ISBN: 9798891264021
eBook ISBN: 9781629898735
First Edition World Castle Publishing, LLC, January 22, 2018
http://www.worldcastlepublishing.com

Licensing Notes

Cover: Karen Fuller
Editor: Maxine Bringenberg

Chapter 1

Lewis had no idea who he'd hired as yet. Nor, and this one frightened him just a little, what they were going to do when they started working. He supposed, like the first group he'd brought on, they'd figure it out among themselves, but he was exhausted. And he was sure that he'd not eaten a decent meal in a month. Taste testing, to him, didn't count.

He looked at his mom when she cleared her throat.

"What can I do?" He took her hand into his and kissed the back of it. "That's very lovely, son, but it's not getting this wedding going. Dalton and Gabe have been very nice in waiting for you to get your feet under you, but I need this, and I want you to let me help you."

"I don't even know where to begin. In the month since I had you guys here to sample my food, I've been running on empty." A plate, a platter really, of food was set before him. "What's this? Mom, I don't think I can taste another bit of food

5

today."

"It's your lunch. Eat, and I'll get the list I have to go over with you." She pulled out a notebook, not a list, and turned it to a page filled with her pretty writing. "Eat, Lewis. I don't have time for you to faint away on me at this point. I need you healthy and happy. Your mate will never forgive me if you're too exhausted to give me grandchildren."

"Mom, I think you should be happy with the ones you have now." She hit him in the back of the head then handed him a fork. "I love you, my dear, but you're a tad on the violent side."

"You drive me there." He took his first bite of food and moaned. "There, you see? Food is just what you need. And there is supposed to be…. Ah, there they are. Biscuits and tea too. Okay. The cake is being made by Emma. Oh my, it's going to be beautiful. Also, flowers are being done by the pack. Some of them can be left here, should you want them."

"I can use them as table toppers. There is a place in the back that was put in for that kind of stuff. Who made this meal?" She said that several of the cooks had put their heads together and done it. "The meatloaf is really tasty, and I think I might use these potatoes too. They have pieces of garlic in them."

He gave his mom a bite of them and she moaned at it. She got up and got a fork, and asked one of the waitstaff that was putting the chairs under the tables to bring her something to eat as well. Lewis asked his mom about the luncheon that she was going to.

"They won't be serving anything but those nasty little sandwiches that I despise. And who can fill up on a slice of cucumber on a tiny piece of toast? No one, I tell you." She was given a plate of food too. "Oh my, Lewis, these green beans are heavenly."

The two of them ate without working on her list. They talked, instead, about the food they were eating. He was going to serve this meal one night and see how the rest of the family liked it. As he was shoving his empty plate away, a serving of cherry crunch was set in front of him. This was his favorite dessert.

Piling whipped cream on it, not even caring that he was already stuffed, he asked his mom about Dalton and his job. Dalton was working for the diner down the street, as well as consulting on crimes that came in. So far there hadn't been much of that going on though. Lewis thought his brother was happy not being stressed all the time.

"He loves it; and Gabe is happy, so that, to me, is all that matters. Are you going to share that, young man?" He thought about telling her no, but she had that look in her eyes that told him the question had been a demand, not a request. "Also, you should know that I went to your house this morning. I have to tell you that I love the work you've had done on it so far. The colors that you've used in the living room, they're very soothing."

"Yes, well, you can thank Kenton for that. He gave me a chart that told him what colors to paint for a soothing waiting area. I don't think he used it. That waiting room of his resembles more of a kindergarten room, with a mixture of adult stuff added in at the last minute." They both laughed. When the crunch was finished, he knew that he was going to have to take a nap, for about a month. "Have you heard much from the others about

Vance?"

"No. He's out doing something I'm sure that he'd not tell me about if he was right in the middle of it." He could see the worry on her face, and regretted bringing it up. "But, he'll be safer now that he has the magic that came with all this. And that, right there, that's what makes it so that I can sleep at night. I worry for all my boys."

"I love you, Mom." She said that she loved him as well. "Well, now that I feel fortified, let's have a go at that list of yours. I do have the linens taken care of. And there is the wholesaler that I got from Gabe, her friend. He's a good guy. And I'm sure that he's getting me the best prices too."

They talked for another hour. It was good to know that he had so much support from his family. Lewis was sure that he'd not be able to make it without them. He just hoped that his mate would be just as supportive and a little like the women already here. His mind drifted a bit when he thought of the conversation that he'd had with Kenton last night.

"She might be more than you want. Just putting that out there." Lewis asked him what he meant. "You know, you're so laid back and easy going. What if she's not? What if she's intense all the time? Like on the go?"

"I guess we'll work it out. Have you all been talking about me and my mate?" Kenton grinned at him. "I see. And what else is being said? Like, will she make me toe the line? Will she be a ball buster like your wife is?"

"My wife is a ball buster, and I love her for it. But you, I worry about you and having a ball buster." Lewis frowned and asked him why he'd say something like that. "I don't know. As

I said, you're so laid back and easy going. I worry that you'll have more clashes than we all did together."

He didn't want to think about clashing with anyone, and Lewis supposed that was his brother's point. Lewis did like things quiet, and he preferred reading over television. It was why the one that he'd bought recently was still in the box. And that the first thing he'd set up to his liking was the library, when he'd put all his books on the shelves. He was a man that liked peace.

After his mom left him, Lewis sent most of the crew home. They would be back in the morning, and they'd practice what they were going to do at the grand opening. But first he had to figure out what he wanted to cook for his brother's wedding that was in four days. It would be huge since Dalton was well known in this town, as well as Gabe had met a lot of the people through her work.

They wanted simple. Food that could be eaten standing up, as well as hot or cold items. The veggie trays were all lined up, ready to be filled, and the wings that Dalton had wanted were in the walk-in thawing out. He was going to make a variety of them, from mild to very hot. His family loved the very spicy.

When he turned to go see what he might need to order extra, he saw the woman standing there. "Can I help you?" She didn't say anything, but he could see that she was ready to take off should he move too quickly. He felt a small invasive touch of his mind, but didn't let her in all the way. He knew it had to be her; everyone in his family knew him better than he did. "Are you a part of the staff that was hired today? I've sent everyone home but a few of the dishwashers. Are you a part of

9

that crew?"

"No. I'm looking for Lewis McCade. I'm supposed to meet him at five o'clock here." She didn't move, didn't look around. Lewis took a step toward her, but when she lifted up a gun, he froze. "Don't come any closer. If you do, I might have to hurt you. As I said, I'm looking for Lewis McCade. Where is he?"

"I'm Lewis." The gun disappeared. Not that she put it away, but it was simply gone. "Who are you and why are you here? If we had an appointment, I wasn't told about it."

"My name is Raven. I don't remember if I had a last name or not, but when pressed, I just use Smith. Not very inventive, I know, but then I don't much care for people as a general rule, so I avoid them. I'm sorry, I'm babbling. Caelin said that I do that a great deal." Lewis asked her if she meant the dragon or the man. "Dragon? No, the man. He's not here yet, but he sent me to find you."

"Why would he...? You're my mate." She nodded and walked toward him. There was something about her that made him see that she was careful where she was walking, and he realized that she was blind. "Can I help you?"

"No. I mean, that's very nice of you, but I use my magic to get around well enough. Unless you push something in front of me when I'm walking, I tend to do all right." She sat down in the chair that he'd been in earlier today. "This is a nice place you have here. I mean, I can't see it, but I can feel it. You've done a good job."

Something touched his head. Not a search this time, but more like a bit of fear, as if he shouldn't be there. Not just in this room, but anywhere this woman was. Fear was there, but

10

he was slightly nauseous as well. A strange combination when one meets their mate, he thought.

"I'm confused." She nodded and told him she was as well. "You just came here? Without the jewelry? Usually we're warned when we have someone coming. Not only something about them, but also which piece they have."

"Oh no, I have it. I've not had to wear it yet because I didn't come here by conventional means. I have the brooch, but I've not worn it, for the simple reason that I cannot figure out how to put it on my clothing. I mean, I'd look really silly, don't you think, if I were to wear it upside down or sideways?" Lewis sat down and told her he'd help her, but he didn't want to touch her. Not even to get close enough to share the same air. "You will, but not today. The second that I put it on, then the others, the men that want it, will come here. Right now, I'm all right with getting to know you and your family. I'm harmless for now."

Harmless? For now? He wasn't sure what that meant, then he thought of what she'd said. Her last name...she didn't remember it. Before he could ask her, even if he wasn't quite sure that he wanted to know, she stood up and put her hands in front of her.

"I'm a witch. Or, I suppose you could call me a little of everything. Black and white witch, and a little faerie as well as some brownie. My mother was a very powerful and beautiful witch. My father...well, not as nice nor as beautiful in his creation." He nodded, but realized too late that she couldn't see him. "Please stand up, Lewis. I should like to get to know you a little."

11

He wasn't sure what to do. Any thoughts he had of letting this woman be near him seemed to double his need to back off, to run. Standing up, he didn't feel like this was right, not even a little, but when she reached out to touch him, just to put her hands on his face, he felt himself getting sicker, as if he wasn't able to hold down his lunch. So, taking another step back, he reached for his family.

Something is off. A lot. My mate, or someone that says that she's my mate, is right here in the room with me. And I locked up, now that I remember, so how did she get in? But I'm feeling sick by the thought of her touching me. Dragon told him to get away, and before he could think that was a wonderful idea, he thought of the dragons. *Come to me, my babies.*

As soon as they entered the room with him, he felt better, stronger even. They didn't move other than to stand in front of him, but they were staring at Raven like they weren't sure either. Then it occurred to him. She was backing up as well.

"You shouldn't be able to call them to you as yet." He asked her why not. "Because, you have no mate."

"I thought you said you were my mate." She took another step back, and Lyna moved to stand behind her. "You cannot leave here until I get some answers. Who sent you?"

"Call them off, Lewis. I'm not kidding around here. Call them off now." Lewis shook his head. "Call them off and I'll be on my way. Perhaps it was a mistake. I'm not your true mate. Maybe I'm mate to your other brother. That's it. Just call them off and I'll be on my way."

"I don't think so." He told his family what was going on. *She's standing here backing from them, and the dragons are waiting.*

12

On what, I have no idea, but they're not hurting her.

Maybe you've made a mistake. He told Kenton that he didn't think so. *We're nearly there. Just don't...I was going to say do anything stupid, but that isn't anything you would do anyway.*

Lewis wasn't sure what Kenton meant by that, but the woman in front of him started to move her mouth, to wave her hands in a way that made him think of spells and magic. Roderick went to her and sat upon her shoulder, and when she cried out her mouth stopped, as did the motions with her hands. Black goo started to run from his claws at her shoulder. He knew that he was holding her, but he didn't know why.

"Roderick, is she who she told me she was?" He shook his head, and Lyna landed on her other shoulder, taking the woman to the floor. Whatever was going on, they were unsure as well. "Is she my mate?"

"No, my lord, she isn't who she says." He asked him to explain. "She is.... Shall I show you who she is?"

"Yes, please, but don't let her go." In seconds the woman was gone, and in her place was a creature that he had no idea what to even guess it was. "What is that?"

"It is very old, sir. A shifter. Not like you have here, in this time frame. This is very old, like the person who made it has less magic, but what it has is all black. This thing isn't like your shifters, but one that can take on the appearance of anything that it is ordered to. May I check its mind?" Lewis nodded just as his family filled the room. "It was hired by King Butler. Its job was to come here, kill you and the rest of the family, then to take what did not belong to them."

"You keep calling it an 'it'; does it have no gender?" Lewis

13

wasn't sure why that mattered until Grady continued. "I mean, by it being called an it, can we assume that it would be able to be anything. A car, an...I don't know, something else that might kill him?"

"No, but that is a good reasoning. No, it can only take on the appearance of something that is alive, with a heartbeat." Lewis asked Roderick if that meant his mate was still alive. "Yes. If she were dead, then this creature could not assume her identity. I can tell you more should you wish it."

"Yes, please. Tell us whatever you've found out." Lewis sat down while Roderick told them what he'd been able to find out. His knees just simply gave out on him as he fell more than sat. His mom came to sit by him and he just looked at her.

"My mate is alive and coming." She nodded and asked him if he was all right. "I am, I think. I've...I was willing to let her touch me. To kill me. Does that mean that I'm too trusting?"

"No. I think that she was very good at convincing someone that she was who she said she was. I wonder if what she told you, the part of her being blind, is true to your mate." Mom turned and asked Roderick, and Lyna answered.

"Yes, my lady. Raven is blind, but she is much more beautiful than this hag has portrayed her as being. Long dark hair, beautiful skin that is kissed by the sun. She spends a great deal of time in the daylight." Lewis wasn't sure it was good for him to have more information, but he thought it might help him. "When she arrives, she will come to you and know who you are. Raven is a witch, and a powerful one. She has been practicing for a great many decades."

"Her last name...does she have one?"

14

Lyna said that she went by Wood. Her name was Raven Wood. "She is on her way here, my lord, and when she arrives, she will deal with this creature."

"Why?" Everyone nodded at his question. "I mean, can't you two take care of it? I don't want to assume that you can or can't, but why wait on her?"

"This is a creature of black magic. To kill it, we would receive the magic that it holds. Black magic." He didn't know what that meant, but she answered for him. "Black magic is tainted. We are white. If we kill it, then our magic would also be tainted. With the power of the one who created it."

"King Butler created this one." They both nodded. "I see. So how do we contain it? So that when Raven gets here, it can be taken care of."

"We can hold it as we are now, but to do so would make it so that only one of us is ready to come to you. I should like to suggest that the creature be put into a place that it cannot escape from." Lewis was almost afraid to ask. "Do you, perhaps, have a glass jar? One that has a metal lid?"

He stood up and went to the sink. He'd just that morning emptied out a large pickle jar. He was drying the pickles so he could deep fry them for the staff. Not even bothering to rinse it out, he held it open while Lyna and Roderick picked the thing up and hung it over the jar. With a sudden popping sound, the creature was inside and the lid closed.

A blackish cloud moved around the jar staring at him, then eyes first being side by side then one under the other. It was sort of sickening, watching it, and he put a towel over it to hide it from his sight.

15

Lewis put the jar and the creature that had meant to kill him on a shelf in the back of the restaurant. It would have killed him, too, if he hadn't smelled something so vile that it made him ill. He wanted to ask someone what it meant, and he would, but right now, all he could think about was that he might well have died had it not been for the dragons.

"She made me sick." The words, not meant to be said just then, slipped from his mouth. He looked at the tiny dragons when they didn't say anything. "When she was close enough to touch me, I could smell something...I think it was evil. I don't know how that happened."

"Evilness is something that all creatures of black magic, black magic, can smell. I have never heard of a dragon being able to smell such a thing, but you might have gained that ability from Raven." Lewis pointed out that he'd not seen her yet. "No. But that doesn't mean that she isn't protecting you from afar, my lord."

She wasn't even near him and she was already protecting his ass. How stupid would she think he was when she got here? he wondered. Feeling slightly put out, he told everyone that he was fine now and that they should go home. Lewis thought they'd seen enough of his failure for one day. When they were gone, none of them very happy with him he thought, he sat down again.

"My lord?" He told Warrior that he wasn't in the mood to talk right now. *Yes, I can understand that, but you have nothing to be ashamed of.*

"Don't I? I nearly got myself killed because I didn't think before acting." Warrior pointed out that he had called the dragons. "Yes, to save my ass. I'm not sure this is going to work with this woman, whoever she is. She's blind and I'm stupid. Stupid enough to nearly get myself killed. What a pair we're going to make, don't you think?"

When Warrior started to speak again, he told him he'd had enough for one day. Going out to his car after locking up, he sat there for several minutes, trying to wrap his mind around his life right now. He had a mate coming soon, probably on her way, and he was, in a way, just as blind as she was.

Pulling into his drive and entering his house, he could see that the workers had gotten a lot done today. The walls were up in the dining room where he had enlarged it. The windows had arrived for the kitchen just yesterday and they had been put in, and some of the cabinets were already in place. He loved his home even though he was redoing a great deal of it, but he wondered what his mate would think when she got there.

"Nothing, you moron, she can't see it." He was having himself a full out pity party, and hated himself for it. As he wandered around the house, looking at what had been accomplished, he kept going back to how the thing had tricked him. How easy it had been for it to do so. He wondered if Butler thought the same thing, that he was easily duped.

"Yes, and why wouldn't he? You've had it pointed out to you on several occasions that you're laid-back. I wonder now if they were all thinking that I'm a fool." He didn't really think that, he supposed, but his pity party wouldn't be complete without him thinking the worst of his family, now would it?

What is going on in your head? Lewis smiled when he heard the voice of his mother. *I swear to you, Lewis, if I wasn't in bed now*

17

and trying to read my new book, I'd come over there and give you a good pop to the head. What is the matter with you?

I nearly got myself killed today. She said that he hadn't, so that's what he should be thinking about. *Mom, we're so close to having this end, and I nearly made it all have to start again.*

Lewis, you didn't. You used your smarts and called for help. To me, that makes you the smartest man I know. Yes, you could have easily died, but you have to remember something son…you're immortal. He hadn't thought of that, and told her. *Yes, well, how do you think you got to be so smart? Now, go to sleep and we'll have breakfast together. You and me. I'm in the middle of a good part, and I'd like to finish this tonight. I love you, son.*

I love you too, Mom. And you are brilliant. She told him she knew that and to hush. Laughing, Lewis headed to his bed and closed his eyes. He was an immortal.

Chapter 2

Butler moved about his hovel. He should have known that his son would be fucking around with his plans. He'd been doing so since he'd been found out. He was king, by the gods, and Caelin should have respected his wishes, not tried to thwart them. To have a son that was so much like his mother was something that stuck in his craw like a bad meal. No, worse, it was like having a knife in the belly.

He looked down at the wound that would fester at times, making him so ill that he couldn't move out of his own bed. His son had done that. Just threw him to the ground and run him through. The wound even now gave him pains, but at least for the moment, it was no longer seeping out the black goo that he knew was his blood.

"Damn him to hell." Getting to the window was no easy feat for him. He'd suffered a great many wounds over the years, and they were coming back to haunt him. The magic that he had gotten easily enough was now in short supply. Not just to him, but to all that were looking for easy pickings. "No one believes in magic as they used to."

It was true. Even the kids of the world, they seemed to prefer having their heads stuck deep into some sort of machine rather than looking at the magic that was right there before them. And witches were either no longer around, not much anyway, or they were getting better at hiding from him. He still wanted to find the one that had made him immortal. She took more than she should have when she'd helped him.

The magic she'd given him had come with a price for them both. Hers could be returned to her, but his, the thing that she'd done to him, would soon take him under. He only had a few more weeks on his immortality, and that was just not enough time for him to do all that he needed. Once he ruled the dragon he'd be immortal like it was, but now, without having all the pieces, his days were numbered. She had put that little part in there when she'd agreed to help him.

"Well, help was not really what she did for me, now was it?" He laughed a little. "The next time that I see the wench, she'll pay with more than just her sight, she will. To think that even tied up the way she was, she still did me wrong. Her king; I'm her fucking king."

Raven. As black as the bird she was named for. He laughed a little more as he watched the road before him. People were always in such a hurry now. And once they got to wherever they were going, they had to wait again. He thought that when he was king once more, he'd take all the devices that seemed to rule everyone and destroy them. That way they'd only have him to come to when they wanted information. His mind drifted to Raven again.

Blind now, she should have been easily found. How many blind old women could there be that lived on their magic? None that he could find, nor the idiots that worked for him. Butler wondered if she had died, been killed by someone that she'd double crossed, but he knew she'd be more careful than that. Raven, for all her evilness, was the greatest witch, besides his own wife, that he'd ever known.

The place he was staying had been abandoned many years ago. He'd been a fool when he'd first happened upon it, making the inside of the place much nicer for himself. Expanding the walls, covering them in the most beautiful of damasks and paintings. The furniture was of the finest woods, beautiful sheens to them. Even the plates that he ate from had been made of gold and silver.

The house appeared ready to fall down, but once you entered his domain, it looked as if a king had lived there, one such as himself. But no more. Everything that he'd put inside, it was gone. The magic wasn't there to support such things.

When his magic had started to deplete, so had the things he'd made. Now he was reduced to having a single nice room, and that too was falling down around his ears. Just last evening his table that he had lorded over by himself had fallen over, taking the little bit of food he'd stolen with it.

He made his way back to his chair and sat upon it. There wasn't time for self-pity. There were things going on that he needed to be stopping. The McCades, they were very close to getting what he wanted…to rule the dragon. He wondered where his shifter was.

"That cost me. Making that thing work for me, it surely did cost me." He wondered if it had done its job, and if he was even now going to have to start anew to get the pieces that he needed since it had killed one of the McCades. The one he had, the necklace, was going to rule for him. And the sooner they figured that out, the better it would be for them.

Opening his shirt, he looked at the piece that he'd had for so long that it felt like a part of his body. Since his last wife had been put into her early grave, he'd worn it around his neck so that no one, not a single person, could take it from him. He even bathed with it on him. And that once a week ritual was scary when it was as exposed as he was.

Calling to the shifter, he was met with nothing. He could have assumed that it had done its job and died, as it was supposed to do, but with his luck, which had been terrible of late, the thing was still trying to find its way to the McCades.

Butler hadn't a clue which man it was going to find. All it had to do was go to the sleepy little town, find one of them whose mind it could read, and then kill him. He wasn't even sure if it would know his mate's name yet, but the thing could work around that. Just get close, that's all he needed to do, get close enough to kill the man, then disappear. No one would be the wiser.

The sudden pain in his belly had him jerking upright and standing. He looked around for the cause of such a pain.

"Hello, Butler." The mist before him laughed. He couldn't make out who it was, but Butler was sure he knew the voice. "Of course you know me. I'm very hurt that you do not recognize me."

"Prisane? What are you doing around here? I thought you dead by now." He had no idea if she could even die, but when she came into focus, all he could do was stare at her. "Christ, woman. That must have surely cost you. You're as beautiful as you were all those years ago."

"You never noticed, so do not try and charm me now. I will not fall to your ways. And magic is mine for the taking, you are right on that, but I have no need to take for me to look as I always have. I am an immortal, like you are not." He sat down and held his belly so that she'd not notice that he'd sprung a leak again. "You're dying, Butler. I'm sure you're well aware of that, but, and it gives me such joy to tell you this, you would have died soon anyway. My children's children are gathering their magic, the things that should rightfully have been theirs long ago."

"You seem so sure about that. What if I told you that I have a plan? You, being a woman, you have no concept of planning the way a man does. So this, like all the other times, it will fail." He laughed, and the pain nearly took his breath away. "Be gone with you. I have no time for your begging me to stop."

"Begging you to stop? Oh no, Butler. I wish for you to go on. To keep trying to stop them. It will give my heart such joy. I know that's an odd concept, for you to know joy, but I shall have it when you are nothing but dust beneath their feet." She was suddenly in front of him, and that was when he realized that she was merely an image. "You will die by their hands, and I will come back to live with them."

"Nay, I will not be killed by one of my own." She laughed

and touched her fingers to his belly. The pain was much worse than it had ever been, and he screamed loudly. "Why do you torture me so? What have I ever done to you to deserve such treatment?"

"You need ask? My goddess, Butler, you were beyond cruel to me. You beat me, badly, and on our wedded night even. Then you threw me down the stairs when I did not come to you again. Over and over I was treated with pain and ridicule. You are a monster. Now more than ever. But what did you think would happen, Butler? That I would come to you willingly? That I would just turn over all that I was without a fight?" She threw back her head and laughed. "I gave myself a son from our union. One that even now plots your demise. And he will help to kill you; if not him, then he has someone that will."

"You think this, yet you come here to beg." She told him she had not begged him for anything. "No, perhaps not yet, but you shall. I will have our son at my mercy, and I will end his life. You should have given him over to me, Prisane. It was wrong of you to raise him without my guiding hand. He is... well, he is now nothing more than a bastard son to me."

"Yet he is your only son. I took care of that too, did I not?" He hated her then. Butler always had, but at this moment, had she really been there, he would have killed her. "You cannot kill me anymore than you could have long ago. Not only am I smarter than you, but I am stronger."

With a wave of her hands, his home took on the appearance of something grand. The tapestries on the walls were the ones he'd stolen off the very walls in her castle so long ago that they were mere rags now. The grand chairs were sitting atop a dais, just as beautiful as they'd been long ago. And when he looked at the table set before him, a long wooden plank of a thing, he could see golden goblets, trenchers made of the finest woods. Even silverware that had not been used when he'd been in the castle gleamed on the table next to the finest of linens.

Food appeared then. Large platters of turkey and ham, vegetables that he knew were as fresh as they could be. Tankers of fine mead and wines. Even cookies, his favorite, were laid at each place setting, and his mouth watered for just a taste.

Then the men and women appeared, their faces blurred enough that he couldn't make them out. Their laughter rang through the room; joy was being had, and he could see that there were so many of them that he couldn't count them past ten. Butler looked at his wife of long ago.

"See them there, Butler? My family. They are happy. Together and rich beyond even what you were when you came to my castle. It will rise again, this I promise you, and when it does, when they are all together, no one will think of you, thank you for giving life to my son. They will raise their glasses to me and all that I have given them." He told her she lied. "You know as well as I that I cannot lie. Not to you or anyone. I am a great white witch, and you are nothing."

The room returned to its former slobbery. He sat down again, his body drained a bit more from the loss of it all. And when Prisane laughed he looked at her and saw something that he'd never seen before. She was wearing all the jewels.

"How is that possible?" She touched the ring on her finger, the necklace at her throat. "You cannot have those. They were sold off, long ago."

25

"You see what I want you to see, Butler. This will be the last time that you see them all together too. For, very soon now, you will meet with the family and you will die. Die as you should have long ago."

After she was gone, he sat there staring at nothing. And there wasn't anything, either. His castle, the one that he'd made, was now gone. All the magic that he'd used had been taken when she left. Cursing her, yelling out that he was going to destroy her, weakened him, and he made his way to the ticking on the floor. Even his bed was gone. Butler needed to rest, then he was going to find the McCades and kill them himself.

Waking in the middle of the night, he laid there for several moments, afeared that Prisane had returned to take more from him. But there was nothing about that he could see, so he sat up slowly. There was a small bit of light coming from the room next to him, and he dreaded going to see what it could be. It would be his luck that he'd left a candle burning, and even now his home was going up in flames.

The little light wasn't a candle, but magic. Getting closer to it, he knew that whoever had left the note had known that he could not read. As he made out the pictures drawn there, he touched his fingers to the corner of it, only to move it closer when it came to life. Stepping back, he watched the shifter he'd sent being destroyed.

There was no hope for the thing. Whoever had bottled it up, they had known what they were about. And the magic that had destroyed it, powerful magic, had snuffed out the life that he'd given it, and he knew a kind of fear that he'd not felt in decades. Then the voice started speaking to him.

"The next time you send someone to do your dirty work, you should be more careful of what they smell like." He didn't know what that meant, but waited. "Evil, your kind, has a scent to it, and that is what gave your magic away."

Evil had no scent, at least not that he'd ever been aware of, but when the message that had been left disappeared along with the light, the room that he was in simply vanished. He found himself standing in the middle of a field with the house, now nothing more than splinters of wood and dirt, lying about.

Butler wanted to sob. To just lay his head down and cry like a small child. He could not go on like this much longer, he knew this, but if he didn't go forward, finish this job, he'd be destroyed, just as she had warned him he would. But there was something that she didn't know, that no one knew, save him. He had a piece to the set, and he wasn't going to give it up for anything.

~~~

Raven leaned against the large tree and smiled. The fact that it was raining didn't bother her; the grasses and other creatures of the land needed it. She even enjoyed it falling upon her face, cleansing away the dirt and grime from walking as far as she had.

A car would have made it quicker to get to Ohio, but she couldn't drive. A plane would have worked should she have wanted to be there in less than an hour, yet she enjoyed walking, and it was a good way for her to gather some of the things that she would need someday. With her heightened sense of smell, she could find more herbs than someone that could see. She only hoped that her mate, whoever he was, didn't mind that

27

she wanted a room to herself, a place that she could keep up with her magic.

"There is magic all around you, mistress." Raven turned toward her bird, the one that had landed in her bed the day she'd been birthed. It was what she'd been named for. "You must eat soon. Even I can hear your belly telling you that it needs to be fed."

"I am searching for something that will give me energy as well as fill me. There is a fine patch of wild berries just over there, I think." She headed that way now, with Poe on her shoulder. "I should be there tomorrow, early. Have you found me a place to stay that will keep me safe?"

"I have. There are numerous houses that are being worked on in the town that you can use without being seen. But, I should like you to know that your mate, he has a lovely home for the two of you." She asked him how that was possible when she'd not met him yet. "He has it from one of his family members. It is a large house that I think will suit you well. I have also taken the liberty to make it safer for you, as well as the other homes."

"Butler is close, I think. He will have to find them soon enough, or everything that he has been planning will come to an end." Not that she cared about the man…he had made her life a living hell for nearly all her life. "Once I am there, will you please go to see my mate? Not to warn him that I am here, but to see how he is faring."

"He has a shifter." She stiffened and asked him how he'd come to have one. "It is not his, but Butler's. He sent it in your form to kill him. Lucky for him, he could call the dragons to him."

28

"The pair?" Poe told her that was them. "I see. I didn't know that he could call them as yet. I thought they were a part of the necklace."

"Nay, they are a part of all. And the couple that has them, they live upon their bodies until called. A couple of the women are breeding as well, one a dragon. They have been taking care not to be too far from each other, and that is keeping them safe." She sat down near the patch of strawberries and let her hand guide her over the ripest ones. "My lady, do you suppose that when you have your mate, you will have your sight restored?"

"I don't know why that would bring it back, Poe. Do you?" He said that he was hoping. "I will just be his mate, nothing more. And help him when he should need it. But from what I've heard from Lord Caelin, they are doing a good job of staying ahead of Butler."

She knew from Lord Caelin that she would be one of the brides for the McCades. While Raven didn't care to be a wife to anyone, she knew the importance of what was going on, and to just do as told. It wasn't in her nature to be submissive to anyone, but in this, she knew it was what was needed.

"In all the generations that have tried to do this, not once have I been this close to having a mate. There has been no family that has been closer than this one." Poe said that he knew this as well. "Do you think they'll be strong enough to make it so? That the dragon and all the others can be called forth again?"

"I do." She asked him why when she'd had her fill. "The other men were too lazy, if you do not mind me saying so. This family, they have a mother that keeps them in line, but she has also taught them humor and humility. She is what I have heard

29

referred to as stern but gentle. Much like your own mother was."

Her mother had been murdered the day she'd lost her sight. It had been Butler, too, that had taken her life. He'd said he'd only hold her until Raven had done what he wanted, but instead of releasing her, as he had promised, he had murdered her. Removing her head, and then laughing when she lay at his feet.

"He shall pay for that." He hadn't so far, but she didn't say that to Poe. It would do her no good to point out that it had been so long since it had happened that she could no longer remember her mother's face. "When you get to the McCades, do you have a plan, my lady?"

"No. I will be his mate, and from there, I don't know what will happen. For all I know, he could be as bad as his first sire." Poe told her that the two men left without a mate were not like him at all. "We shall see. If he would give me some space to call my own and a little garden, I can be very happy."

"I do not believe that any more than you do. Be happy with a plot of dirt and a little room. You would rather die than to have so little to do with your craft." She laughed at her bird. "I wonder at times if you have your head in the right place. You will make me an old bird soon."

"You are an—"

The forest around them was suddenly quiet. Raven pulled her magic around her as Poe left her side. He could tell her what was about, and she'd have to trust him to keep her safe. Being out in the open this way, it was nothing that she should have done.

"I haven't any idea what you think I'm going to find here." The man's voice, while frustrated, didn't seem to be angry. "You said that you knew where some strawberries were. So far all I have to show for this trip to the woods is a basket of wild clover and a few very sad looking violets."

"I tell you, Uncle Lewis, I was out here yesterday with Aunt Emma, and they were right around here. I'm not sure where, but that tree looks...." She tensed up when the younger voice stopped talking. "What is it, Uncle Lewis?"

"I'm not sure. Ever since that shifter thing came in my restaurant, I have this feeling that everything is wrong. Like that bird there. What the heck is it doing just staring at me?" The young man laughed. "You'd not think it was so funny if it just started talking to you. And just so you know, that's exactly what I think it can do."

"Uncle Lewis, you need to chill out." She put her hand over her mouth when laughter bubbled up. "Birds do not talk. Ravens are really smart, but I don't think they've gotten to speech yet."

"So you say." She felt them grow closer to her and wanted to back up, but knew that they'd see her. "Gavin, I want you to stand very still. Something is here with us. Someone...I'm not sure, but stand still."

She knew who the man was. She also knew who the child was, but that didn't make her feel any better about this. The thought of putting them to sleep so she could run was taken out of her hand when Poe started talking to them both.

"Thank you, young man. I am very intelligent, but I think that has more to do with my magic and age than anything else.

31

I am Poe. Raven to Raven." She felt the earth laugh with her; the man hit the ground and the young boy laughed. "She is here, but hiding. As you can well imagine, it has been a while since we've been able to talk to anyone besides ourselves."

"You're talking." The young boy laughed again as he spoke. "My goodness, you're talking to us, and we can understand you."

"Well, of course you can. Sir, are you unwell?" She let go of her magic at the concern in Poe's voice. She couldn't see the man, but she could feel his fear. It was as if he were wearing it as one would a shield. "This is Lady Raven. Mate, I think, to you, young Lewis."

"No. I don't...I don't trust this." She stood up and bowed before the two of them. "She was here before. Not you, but a person who was pretending to be you. She wanted to kill me. And she would have because I was so trusting."

"The shifter." Poe told her that was correct. "I'm not a shifter. A witch, but not a shifter. If you were to take me to it, I could—"

"No. You're not going anywhere near my family. I don't know anything about you. Or why you're here now." The man was terrified, but it surprised her to realize it wasn't for himself, but for the young man. "Gavin, go back to the truck. And lock the doors. I don't know if that'll help, but you go there now."

"Uncle Lewis—" The young boy was told to go now, but before she could assure him that she wasn't going to harm either of them, the dragons were there. Raven could feel their need to destroy. Then happiness.

Lyna came to her first, and when she sat upon her shoulder,

32

Raven knew that Roderick wasn't far from her. Without moving too quickly, Raven ran her fingers over the hard scales of the dragon. As she did so, she spoke to the man that the earth told her was standing up now.

"They're friends of mine. They would know immediately if I was friend or foe to any of you." He told her that they'd not killed the other thing either. "No, they'd not be able to. Simply because they are white magic, and I am not. I'm neither. But I can destroy it for you, should you want me to."

"I don't know what to think or believe anymore." She could hear it then, his anger at not being informed. Also, his frustrations with himself. "Are you real? I mean, are you the real Raven Wood?"

"I am, and you are Lewis McCade, one of the dragons that is awakening Warrior. I know him as well. Should you ask him, I'm sure that he could tell you. Even the earth, a good friend of mine, she could also tell you." She wasn't upset that he wasn't believing her. Raven knew better than most what it cost to trust someone at their word. "I am the mate to you. You were told by Warrior that I was to come to you."

"Yes. I know that you're blind and that you're beautiful, which you are, and that you have magic." She thanked him. "How did you become blind? I know that's rude, but Warrior told me to ask you."

"I helped Butler, the king at the time, with immortality. He held my mother hostage while I performed the magic. Then after I was finished, making him what he asked for, he killed my mother, a great witch as well, and her blood spilled across my eyes. Because I had a hand in killing her, though indirectly,

I was cursed by my sight being taken away. To me, it wasn't enough for what I did to her."

"He said that you're right, but I'm still leery, if you want to know the truth." She told him that she didn't blame him. "I'm going to stand up now, and walk toward you."

"I know what you're doing, Lewis. The earth, she helps me when necessary. It's the reason that I've been able to get around so well all these years." Waiting for him to come toward her, his shadow fell over her. "You're very tall. A big man too, without any fat on you. And your dragon, he is there now as well. I couldn't feel him before. Are you going to touch me?"

"Yes, if you'd allow it." She put her chin up and waited. "You have a smudge of dirt on your face, and a stain of berries on your mouth. Like you've eaten berries for your meal."

"The strawberries that you were in search of. I'm afraid that I might have eaten them all." His finger was gentle, and she could tell a great deal about him by it. "You cook with herbs. Own a restaurant that caters more to well-dressed people than your brother does at the diner."

"How did you know that?" His hand stopped moving; fear was there again. "Who told you about us?"

"Caelin. He is a friend of mine as well. But, as you can feel my thoughts and memories, I can yours as well." He said nothing, but pulled his fingers from her face. "You are satisfied then?"

"No, but for now, I'm okay with it." She nodded. It was more than she could hope for. "The raven, Poe, he is with you? Will he be staying at the house too?"

"Yes, but he will mostly live out of doors. Is that all right with you?" He took her hand into his larger one and said that he didn't care. "All right then. Are you taking me someplace? To a hotel?"

"No, to my home."

She didn't say anything else as they traveled to his truck. He was kind to her, not allowing her to step over fallen branches or trees. And when they were in the big truck, he helped her to buckle in, but he said no more. Raven spoke with Gavin, who had lots to say as she thought of the man beside her.

Chapter 3

Lewis started for home after dropping Gavin off at his home. He wasn't sure this was a good idea. But he also knew, from Warrior, that she was really his mate and that she had the brooch. He'd not seen it as yet, not even asked about it, but he had been told she wore it.

It's on her person, Lord Lewis, but not to her skin. Lewis asked why that made a difference. *I cannot speak with her as well as I can you without it being to her skin. Should you ask her to —*

I'm not going to ask this stranger where she has the brooch that she brought to us. I think I've been rude enough to her, don't you? And he had been. But instead of telling her he was sorry, as he knew that he should, he stretched his neck and thought of all the things he was going to do when he dropped her off. *That bird, is it all right for it to be out? I mean, with the magic that it has, will anyone trace it to her?*

No. She is very powerful, and has kept them both hidden away for some time now. Raven will need to be shown the house. If you drop her off, she will not know where things are. He cursed and then told Raven he was sorry. *You are not happy with your mate?*

I don't know what I am. I've had enough going on the last few days that I'm sort of in shock. This isn't like the other mates. I mean, she came here without any assistance, and she's magical. Like stronger than us, magical. Warrior told him that she was also just a woman. *Don't do that. I'm dealing here the best that I can.*

"If you were to talk to me, I'm sure that I can answer any questions that you might have." He looked at Raven when she spoke. "You're upset, I can understand that, but if you would talk to me, perhaps we can get to know each other."

"You were told about the shifter. Were you told what it did to me?" She said that she knew now, that Poe had told her. "He's just a wealth of information, isn't he?"

"You're very snarky, and rude. Your mother, does she know how you act when she isn't around to keep you in line?" He shook his head, then said no. "You should be leery, I agree with that, but there is no cause for you to be nasty to me. I'm just as much upset about things as you are. I'm a very old witch, much older than you might guess. Set in my ways, yet here I am, trying to make the best of this situation that I had nothing to do with."

"I'm sorry." He was too. It wasn't her fault that he was in a crappy mood. "I have so much on my plate at the moment. Not that I didn't want you here, that's not it, but I'm planning a wedding, having a grand opening of the restaurant, as well as having someone new in my home. Our home."

"Thank you." He nodded as they pulled into the driveway.

38

"This house, it's been enhanced. Poe was afraid that I would be located, so he came here and spread more magic over what is already there."

"My family is close by. If he can, do you think that he could do it to their homes as well?" She said it had been done. "Thank you. And I'm very sorry, as I said, I've not been in the best of humor lately. Mostly it's because I'm overwhelmed about a couple of things. You, mostly, but now that you're here, I think that part will calm down. Also, I should have said it earlier... I'm very sorry about the loss of your mom. I don't know what I'd do without mine."

"She was all I had. My father, he wasn't a good man." She opened the door and he got out on the other side. "I can tell what is out here, but once we're in the house, if you could guide me around, telling me where things are, then I should be all right for you to leave."

"No. I mean, that was my plan, but I'm not going to do that. But you might be surprised to find that the house is mostly empty of bigger furniture. I've been filling it with pieces that I like, so if there's anything you want or want to change, let me know." She only looked at him. "I'm sorry. I guess you'd not know if it matched or not, would you? I'm doing this badly."

"No, you're doing very well, and I can tell what the pieces that you have in the rooms are because of my magic. Not size or color, but where it might have started and who made it. Perhaps even who might have owned it. You can do that too." He wasn't so sure that would come in handy as a chef, but she just smiled at him.

"You're very beautiful. I was told that you would be, but

you're much prettier than I dreamed you'd be." She thanked him as they entered the big hall. "This is where I'm having trouble with furniture. Well, the whole house really, but I don't know what sort of things should be in here. Mom told me to put in a table, but that seems so lame."

"Give me your hand, please." He put his hand into hers again and felt the warmth of her all the way to his toes. Also, her magic. "Now, you look around and I'll see what you do. I cannot do this with anyone else, but as my mate, I can see what you do."

"Okay. We'll go slowly. Some of the workers are still here, and I don't want them to trip you up with wires and things that they're using." She nodded, and he led her into the front room. He looked around with fresh eyes, thinking that she was going to see what a failure he'd been at this so far.

"You've enlarged the dining room." He told her how he had five brothers, their wives, his mom, and nieces and nephews too. "I know of a man who works with wood. He has a design for a table that can expand easily enough for your entire family or just a few of them. If you'd like, I can have him come see you."

"Yes, I'd like that. I have some wood that was left over when the house was remodeled. I think the plan had been to cover the barn in old siding, but that failed for some reason." She said that he could work with anything. "Good. This is the way to the kitchen. The most work is going on in there."

She asked him questions and he answered what he knew. Her suggestions for this room were good; put in a little greenhouse off the kitchen area for his own herbs. He was having a walk-in freezer and refrigerator put in as well, but she said that he should put them into an addition to the house with its own power. So if the electricity ever went out, he'd still have his food.

"I should do that at the restaurant as well. That way we won't have too much food loss if the power goes out to the building." He felt better as they went into his office. "I have lots of books along the walls. None of them in braille, I'm afraid, but I do have a computer that can read to you if you'd like that."

"Oh yes. I'd love that. I have one of those reader things that I use. I have read all the great classics, as well as heard a few movies too. You don't watch television, do you?" He told her that he preferred to read, but had been known to sit and watch movies in bits and pieces. "Yes, I've done that as well. I do find that I miss some important plot changes when I do that. It makes for a different feeling when you don't know all that's going on."

Lewis took her to the bedrooms that were empty first. He didn't want her to think he was rushing her to their bedroom. Not that he didn't want her...something about her made him think of lazy afternoons making love all day, and then holding each other. He'd never been much of a person who snuggled, but with her, he thought that might change as well. When they entered the master bedroom, he told her what was in the room.

"I have some furniture too. Not as much as would be needed to fill this house, but things that I have collected over the years. For now, it's in storage because of where I live." He asked her about that. "I live in a house that is built into the mountain. It's warm in the winter and cool in the summer months. And I have

41

fresh water too when needed."

"I bet it's lovely. With the wild things around you as well as the trees. I've not lived here very long, but there are a few animals around. I did have the furnace replaced, as well as the air conditioner to make it nicer in here. The house was in good shape, but just a little outdated. Of course, as you know, I enlarged a couple of the rooms too." She nodded as she wandered around the room, picking up things and then setting them back down. "You said that you could tell about things with a touch. What do you feel when you do that? I mean, do you feel it or get images?"

"Both. Like with this framed picture. I know that you and your brothers are in it. That it's not a recent picture. Your mother took it. None of you were happy about having it taken, I don't think." He said it was the day his father died. "You are sad because of that?"

"No, hardly. He tried to kill me. My mom, she shot him in the head while he held me down with a boot at my neck. His plan was to make my mother heel to him or he would remove my head. So she shot him. I think that I was feeling guilty about that, and my brothers felt badly for our mom too. I know I did." He picked up the picture that she was talking about. "None of us wanted to be at his funeral. We wanted to take Mom home, pamper her, and then celebrate. He'd been a monster for a long time before this."

"Much like Butler." He put the picture back as she spoke of the man that had started this all. "Butler wasn't a good man, ever, and a worse king. I was friends...well, not friends, but I knew his wife. Prisane was a good queen. A nice person, and she provided well for us all. I was her magical assistant. Not that she needed me…she was already powerful, but she let me help her in ways that we both learned from. Butler never took her magic or her very seriously. He thought her just a female. And one who should bow before him in all that he wished."

"She had his son and hid it away from him. That must have been hard for her. Warrior told us how she had turned him into a human for a time to help her." Raven nodded and said nothing more. "How did you get your name? It's very beautiful."

"When I was born, it was storming badly. As I was laid in my crib, the woman who had helped my mother with the birthing said that I should be called that, Rain. But almost as soon as she finished the words, Poe came in to sit upon my bed." She laughed, and Lewis felt the tug of his own laughter too. "He never left me. Even when mother nursed me, he was there, squawking and making a ruckus. So when I was old enough to have my magic come to me, I made it so he could speak. I don't think he's been quiet since then."

As he showed her around the rest of the house, he told her of his restaurant, as well as the things he had planned for it. Telling her how he'd gotten the home they were now in, how little he'd paid for it, as well as owning shops that he was working to get moving as well. She seemed shy to him, and he found he wanted to bring her out of that shell. So when he took her to the back yard, he was surprised when she bent at the waist and pulled a small plant to her nose.

"Rosemary. It's very fragrant, isn't it?" He said that it was, he loved to use it when he cooked. "I dry it and keep it for spells. Nothing bad, mind you. Just a few sleep potions, as well

43

as a salve for wounds."

"Do you have a place to dry them? I mean, I'm assuming that you did. You should have a garden here too. I've been reading up on what witches might need, trying to get our home ready for you, and other than a few things, I didn't find much other than a garden was your treasure." She smiled at him, and Lewis felt like he'd been kissed by the sun in a wonderfully amazing way. "You smile at me like that and I might even buy you a tractor."

"I'd not be able to plow it in straight rows, I'm afraid." When she laughed, he did as well. Her joke was just off the cuff, like she'd only done it to make him laugh with her. Lewis touched her cheek and she leaned into his hand. "You are such a warm and caring person, aren't you, Lewis? I think that I could happily live with you for the rest of our days."

"I'd like that too." He wanted to kiss her, to taste what he could of her, but Poe took that moment to come to them and sat on the ground before them. "Something wrong?"

"Yes, my lord. There are people on their way here. Not your family. I have gone to see them. But this person it is not one that would be associated with Butler either." The gravel crunching in the drive had him pushing Raven behind him. "They don't have evil in their hearts, but I do not trust that either."

"You said that you've met my family." Poe nodded. "Are they all right? None of them have been injured or taken, have they?"

"No, my lord. They are well and hearty. You mother, she is most upset with me, however. I startled her when I was talking to young Gavin. A delightful young boy, he is." Lewis raised

44

his hand and Poe stopped talking.

"Could you make sure that Raven gets in the house? And I know that—"

"I'm not leaving you." He told her it might be dangerous. "Yes, it might, but we're stronger together than we are apart. Just let me put the brooch on."

He watched her as she pulled it from a purse like thing that she had on. The long strap of it was made of leather; the bag itself was worn, but decorated with beads and stones. As soon as the brooch was in her palm, Lewis wanted to touch it, just to feel the magic that there was, and when she put out her hand with it in it, he took it from her and put it on her blouse, right at the opening of it so that it touched her skin.

The magic that settled over him was warm. It was as if he'd been chilled before and someone had put a heavy blanket over him. Taking her hand into his, he walked to the front of the house and nearly told her again to go hide when he saw who was there. This man had been giving his family trouble for a few weeks now, and today wasn't going to be any better.

Reaching for his family, he told them that Byron Clayton was here. The cursing had him laughing, and then his mom spoke to them all. He knew that Raven could hear them too when she smiled at her response.

While I don't usually like that sort of language, Kenton, I think that with this man, it is warranted. What does he want now? Us to turn over all our deeds to the buildings downtown? Lewis said that he'd not spoken to him as yet. *Well, you be careful, son. You have a mate coming.*

She's here, with me. No one spoke, and he knew they were

45

shocked. *She and I were using this quiet time to get to know each other. If you guys come over, you can talk to her too. I think, Mom, that you met Poe, her raven, not long ago.*

I did. Nearly scared a decade off my life. So that's her bird, is it? Well, we'll have to talk about his manners when I see her. His mom laughed. *But one thing at a time. We're on our way, son.*

As soon as Byron saw him, he knew that he was going to be trouble. Byron told them that he had someone with him, a man in a uniform, but Lewis couldn't see what sort of service he was from. His family said they were nearly there. He thought it funny when Raven rolled up her sleeves, like she was ready to mop the floor with the man's head. Poe landed on his shoulder but didn't speak. He supposed not everyone would be as accepting of a talking raven as they'd been.

~~~

Byron hated that he had to come out here and talk to this man. But since Lewis wasn't answering his phone, nor was he accepting the certified letters that he sent him, he decided enough was enough and he'd have to talk to him face to face. Williams, a man that owned a large operation that dealt with bodyguards and such, was with him in the event that Lewis got smart with him. Which Byron really hoped that he did.

"Lewis. That's a little strange, even for you, isn't it?" Lewis asked him what he meant. "You have a crow on your shoulder. I knew that you were eccentric, but I didn't think you were that much." He laughed, but Lewis didn't. "I was joking, young man. Where is your sense of humor nowadays?"

"With you? I have none. And it's a raven, not a crow. What is it you want, Clayton? I think I've made it clear that I've no

46

desire to sell you that building." Byron nodded and reached for his wallet. "I don't know what you think you might be doing. But you reach for anything in that pocket again, I'll have you down on the ground in a second."

"You're awfully hostile today. Are you showing off for the pretty lady here? It's not like him, honey, to be so—" He had no idea how it had happened, but he found himself not only down on the ground, but in a great deal of pain. When he saw the shoes of Lewis in front of him, he wondered what the fuck Williams had done.

"I want you to meet my wife, Raven McCade. She doesn't like to be called honey, nor, and this makes me so happy, does she like the bullshit that you're tossing around. Now, I'm going to have her let you go, but you are going to state your business, I'm going to refuse you, again, and then you're leaving." He asked him why he'd not sell. "I don't want to."

He was released. When he stood up, Raven moved to stand beside Lewis, who wrapped his arm around her. Byron hadn't heard he'd gotten married. Not that it mattered to him, but he wanted that building. Before he could try again to get him to sell, a few cars pulled into the driveway, and all his family just seemed to pour out of them.

Byron was afraid of their mother. She was hell on wheels, as his own mother used to say. When she had something to say, you listened. While she wasn't mean about it, she did make her point any way that she could. He backed up when she stood in front of him.

"What are you doing here? I thought you've been told that you are not going to get that building. Several times, as a matter of fact." He opened his mouth to speak, but she cut him off. "Lewis and the rest of us are getting mighty sick of you coming around every day to see if we want to sell. We do not. Now, be on your way."

"I had no idea that you owned it with him." She crossed her arms over her chest and tapped her foot. "Maybe you and I should talk. Perhaps you can convince him to sell to me. It's a lot of money to turn down, if you ask me, and the building has some sentimental value for me."

"Yes, we heard you telling us that. But after doing a lot of research on it, it's funny, but your family name never shows up. Not even any cousins, or anyone else that might be related to you. So, come up with a better one, Byron Clayton. That story is getting as old as I am."

His anger at these people spiked and he took a step toward the old woman, and stopped when he heard the voice behind him.

"Touch her and you'll never be able to use either of your arms again. I will yank them from your body and beat you to death with them." He put his hands behind him and the man laughed. Byron was reasonably sure that it was Kenton...he was the only one not in front of him right now. "Good boy. Now, you've been told several times that we're not selling to you. I think you should take that as gospel. Get into your fucking car and get off this land. And if we catch you around any of us again, I'll sic the pack on you. And you know that I can."

He looked at the tree line and saw them, perhaps fifty of them, then, as one, they moved forward, and he could see that his first number wasn't even close. He thought that there were well over a couple of hundred wolves with their teeth bared, for him to have no doubt they'd attack if any one of the McCades said the word.

"Look, I think we've gotten off on the wrong foot here. I am willing to pay you just about anything you want for the building. What can you want it for anyway? I mean, you own everything else in the district, don't you? What is one less building for you?" Lewis asked him what he was going to do with it if he were to own it. "Now, that wouldn't be very good, would it, if I gave over all my ideas for the place? Let's just say that I do have big plans for it."

"No." He opened his mouth to say more, but Lewis turned to the pack and Byron knew that they were finished. "Don't return, Clayton. And I'm giving you fair warning now, as soon as you leave here, I'm going to call the police and have a restraining order put on you. I've tried to be nice about this, but you've pushed me too far. You're going to regret if it you return here again."

"Are you threatening me, Lewis?" The woman next to him laughed. "You think this is so funny? What if I told you that he was turning down millions of dollars by not selling to me? You don't think that's so funny now, do you?"

"I'm sure that Lewis doesn't need the money, especially not yours. And even if he did, I have plenty enough for the two of us to live out the rest of our lives and never touch the principle, just live off the interest. Do I think it's funny? Yes, it's very funny if you think that's the way to get anyone to do anything for you." She put out her hand and touched his. "You're not a good man, Mr. Clayton, and you'll soon be found out."

She knew. He didn't know how she knew or even how much, but she knew enough to scare the shit out of him. Turning to his car, he stumbled twice getting to it. When Williams seemed to linger a little too long for his tastes, he laid on the horn to get him moving. He needed to get away, to think about what was going on. Clayton was all the way to the main road when he had to pull over and get out of his car to puke.

"Christ. They were going to have me killed." Williams leaned against the car and said nothing. "Did you hear them threaten me? They were going to have those wolves kill me."

"Yes, but it's no less than you deserve." He looked at the man and asked him what the fuck he was talking about. "First of all, he's told you no. Secondly, he told you no several times. And this is the real kicker...you were going to hurt their mom. Now, mine would have called the cops on you had you done what you did to theirs. But Mrs. McCade would have whooped your ass all over that yard and back again without even breaking a nail. And had she done that, no one would have ever found our bodies. You don't fuck with the McCades. And had I known that was where we were headed when you asked me to come along, I would have told you no too."

"You're afraid of one little old woman?" He laughed, and Williams just nodded. "They have something that I want, and I'm going to get it."

"Good luck with that, is all I can tell you. But from here on out, you want someone from my firm to go with you, then you're going to be shit out of luck. I like the men that I work with, and I won't have them killed because you have a burr up your ass." Williams started to walk away, but paused and

50

looked back at him. "Here is a piece of advice that I know you won't heed. When you're told that you're to stay away from them, I'd do it. It will save your life. Not might save it, but it will. Those men and women are not ones to fuck with."

Standing there on the side of the road, Byron wondered why they were so set on not selling him that building. It wasn't like they didn't really own the rest of the buildings in that area. And since they'd been putting in shops and having them worked on, the value had gone up a great deal. But the building he wanted, the one that he'd lied about, was going to make him a millionaire. And they were thwarting him in his efforts.

Six months ago, Byron had taken a walk in the merchant district. He'd been trying to cut some of the fat off him, and his doctor had told him that walking was a good way to start. So he'd made his way toward that area and happened to find one of abandoned buildings open. Not quite true…he'd broken the glass and let himself in. But he'd wanted to have a sit down, and thought that he'd find himself a chair inside. And oh, what a treasure he'd found. Not so much on the upper floors—and there were five of them—but down the rickety stairs to the sub levels.

The basement of the place had been filled with all sorts of boxes. Most of them had so much mold on them that he couldn't read the lettering that had been on them, no matter what he'd done. But in the back, well hidden from the rest of the things that had been stuffed down there, he'd found four big assed trunks.

Opening them had been a little more trouble, but when he finally figured out how to cut through the leather along the back, he fell back on his ass, surprised at the contents. Money. A great deal of it too. Stacks and stacks of it. Picking up the first few bundles, he knew that he had fallen on one of the best finds that anyone could ever have found. But to get them out of the building had been impossible the next time he went to move them.

The cameras were everywhere now. And if that wasn't bad enough, there were wolves, pack members, wandering around the area like they owned it. Even driving his truck on the roads had gotten him pulled over and questioned. There wasn't any way for him to get the heavy trunks out without anyone seeing him. He'd researched; taking the trunks was against the law, so he decided to buy the building and get them legally. But that hadn't worked either. Now there were signs posted everywhere he walked, when he could, that stated that the place was off limits unless he had a permit. He'd not been able to go back since, but that didn't mean he wasn't keeping an eye on his building. Byron just had to make Lewis, and now his mom, sell it to him. With the amount of money in the place, he wasn't going to have the law come back and bite him in the ass for it.

"He'll have to sell. As soon as I can figure out what he wants, he'll sell it to me." Or, he thought, he'd have to go to extremes. And the way it was going, Byron was going to have to start that part of his plan to get the money.

Chapter 4

Raven sat very still. She wasn't used to having so many people around her all the time. And they were loud…loving, but loud. When Poe came to sit upon her shoulder everyone grew quiet, and she knew that they had turned to look at her. Poe squawked at them.

"He's my friend." Mrs. McCade, Aisha, came to sit by her; her scent was all around her then. She asked if she could touch him. "Yes, if he allows it, but he talks too. If you want to know anything about him, you can ask."

"Yes, I know that he can speak. Scared me today when he did so. But it was my fault too. Gavin had been trying to tell me, and I wasn't having it. But to see him now, with you, it's a lovely thing to have a creature like him with you. My name is Aisha. What's yours?" Poe told her. "A very good, strong name. I'm assuming he's Poe to your Raven, for the book."

"In a way. My mother told me how he came to me when

I was born, and even later in my life. Later, when 'The Raven' was written, I changed his name to Poe, and we've been using it since. It fit us. But I got my name because he came to see me when I was just born. He came in the open window and landed on my bed. He's been with me since. But I gave him the power of speech when I couldn't understand him very well." Aisha asked Raven what he did for her. "He can go ahead of me and scope things out. Find herbs for me by flying over a field. He's very helpful in guiding me around. And now that Lewis is in my life, he'll help him as well."

"What are you, my dear? Not that it matters much, but I would like to get to know you now that you're a part of our family." She told her that she was a witch. "Black or white? Or do you have a preference?"

"I'm both, but only until the dragon comes to save me." She noticed that everyone was sitting now and listening to her by the way the chairs shuffled around, and the talking had all but stopped. Raven figured this was the best time to tell them what she knew and what was going to happen. "I was tricked into helping Butler in becoming what he is today. An immortal. Well, Caelin said that I wasn't tricked, but made to help him, but I did it all the same. I took my own precautions, and that is what is going to help you now. But I didn't do enough, and it is why I've had my sight taken from me."

"I'm afraid that I don't understand. I mean, I do understand why he wanted to be an immortal. He wouldn't have been able to torture us all these years if he'd just done us all a favor and died. But what I don't understand, and perhaps you can help me with this, is why he wants the pieces. He can't control the

54

dragon." Raven smiled. She liked this woman a great deal. "You know something, don't you?"

"Butler cannot control the dragon, you're correct about that. He, however, doesn't know that. Nor does he understand how the magic works that will bring him forth. Only Caelin knows that, and he's not sharing just yet." She waved her hands around, and she knew what they were seeing…the beautiful castle, the way that she remembered it. "Long ago, even before the necklace was broken down, Butler tried to take the castle for his own. But the problem was — and something else that he didn't know — the castle and all that worked there were magical. And when the queen, his first wife, disappeared within the gem that sets in the center of it, the magic went with her."

The castle that she showed them started to fall apart. Not in small increments, but great stones fell…walls rested in the dirt now instead of holding up the others. She moved her hands again to show it as she had been told it looked now. Nothing but stones in a circle, and a couple of walls half gone.

"He picked up the necklace, the last piece of the set, and put it around the neck of his future wife. She was fat with a child, a boy, but the queen was so angry at him she used her magic and cursed her husband. He was only to ever have girl children. No matter how many maidens he took, they all sired him female children. Butler wasn't a man to take the blame himself, so he killed the women when they had birthed." Aisha said that was terrible. "Yes, but he would have killed them anyway. Not that it makes it any better, but their deaths were important to the chain of events that brought you here. With the women dying that he took to his bed, others began to shield themselves against him. Fathers would no longer allow their daughters to marry him. When he began to take what he wanted, it got him into trouble with the laws of that time. There was a time or two when the fathers of daughters would dress them as sons from their birth so he'd not know they were females of an age to marry. That is where I came in."

"You had to help him, you said, because of your mother." She nodded at the person who spoke. "I'm sorry. I'm Emma. Married to Kenton, the oldest."

"Thank you. When I get your voices paired with your names, I'll remember you better. But yes, he took my mother and tied her to a stone. He had a little magic then, but not as much as he believes himself to have now. He wanted to be immortal. That was all he requested, to be able to live for three thousand years. That would have been a great deal of time, since most people, ones who had little to no magic, only lived until they were in their thirty years." Aisha laughed. "Yes, as you can imagine, that isn't the way to request something from a witch. But I think in the back of my mind I knew that he'd kill my mom, so I fixed the spell, just as I'd been told to do, so that he'd live but he could be hurt badly, and that the three thousand years were set in stone. He can live longer, if he can control the dragon within, but he cannot."

"I'm thinking that it will be me that ends his life. I came home as soon as I got this "gift" to find out if everyone received this and what it would mean. But you didn't, did you?" Everyone moved, and she felt her body tense up. The voice was not one she'd heard before, but he seemed to understand, this newcomer. "I'm Vance McCade. I believe that I'm the one that will kill him because of what I received just yesterday. I think it was from Caelin."

"The family sword." He touched his finger to her arm and she felt the power of it. "Yes, you have it. Where has it come to you? I should like to touch if it you'd not mind."

She heard a shuffling of clothing and was asked to stand. As soon as she reached out, she touched skin. But before she could jerk her hands away, she felt the power of the sword and all that it meant to this man. Also, the sorrow of him and his heart. That he was a haunted man...not just in his mind, but that there were people looking for him.

"The sword is made of the finest steel. It is so sharp that it will cut stone in half with the right power behind it. The wording on it has been forged and filled with gold and gems. The pommel, the handle, is wrapped in silks, then in leather that was dried in the castle. It is bound with the maker's blood, the blood of the queen herself." Vance asked her if she'd made it. "Yes, for her son. When he was old enough to wield it, he stabbed his father with it, knowing that to kill him at that time would have meant the death to all who came after it. But he did wound him badly, enough that even now, it hurts him and seeps with his black blood."

"I've not been able to remove it." Raven told him that he could now. "I'm not sure that I want to, to tell the truth. It appeared to me one night in a dream and told me that it was mine. Then when I woke the next morning, I could feel it as a part of my back, embedded into my skin. But in listening to your story, why not wait until he dies? You said that his time was growing short. Why not wait for that?"

"He must die by your hand, Vance. To die otherwise would not end his magic, but only let it go to someone else. A granddaughter perhaps, that might be around. If he is killed with the sword when the time is right, and you'll know it, then the magic that he has gathered, it too will die. But you must get used to its weight and how to use it, for when the time comes, it will only be you that can remove Butler's head. And you will need to do that in order for the magic to be brought back to life for you all." He asked what the magic was. "I don't know. I know that some of it has to do with the castle, but the rest, and there is a great deal of it, I just don't know."

"You said that you gave something more to the spell to Butler. What was it?" Lewis took her hand when he asked her the question. "You're safe here, love."

"As I said, he was going to kill my mom anyway, so I gave him just a little more than he asked for. One of them was that he could no longer enter the castle walls, fallen or repaired. No babe would ever be born from his loins again." Lewis asked her what else. "I took the necklace from him and replaced it with a copy."

Reaching into her magic bag, she pulled it free from the cloth that she'd wrapped it in. She knew what they were seeing. The first time she'd laid eyes on it, she'd been stunned by its beauty, as well as the magic that surrounded it. Until today, no one, not even Caelin, knew that she had it. At least she was almost sure that he didn't. With him, it was hard to believe, now that she'd met this family, that he'd not mentioned it to her over the decades.

"The last woman, how will she get here if the necklace isn't found by her?" She started to speak, to tell Kenton that she was already on her way, when he spoke again. "No, don't tell me. I'm sure that there is a plan in place for that as well. But with us having all the pieces now, can we not just bring the dragon here and be done with this?"

"No. The women that holds the pieces must complete the dragon. They're the key to the magic. The McCades are the strength of it, but the women, all of us, are what brings the magic out so that he can live here." With another wave of her hand, she showed them what she'd seen so long ago in a dream. "This is the dragon that you seek. He isn't like any other dragon ever born. He was good and kind. His magic was more than anyone ever knew was there for them. And the queen, your queen, gave him more to keep him as her warrior. Warrior is the very first dragon ever. His magic, along with the queen's, is what made the magic for us all to use."

"Why?" She looked in the direction of the voice, but knew that it was Gavin. "I understand some of this. The magic that brings the dragon. The women having to be a part of it. I get that. But why do you need the dragon here? I'm not saying that he shouldn't be, but why is it so important that we bring it out of the jewelry?"

"It's a good question, young Gavin. The dragon, all dragons, are magical. They're the ones that granted it to us. That made witches what they are. Brownies and faeries alike are only here because of the dragon and his magic. Yes, the queen gave him more, but they shared what he had, as well as enhanced what he was, so that they were powerful."

"So, it's more of a chain of events that have to happen in the right order for it to finish." Raven nodded at him, happy that he understood. "That's one of the reasons that it's failed before, isn't it?"

"Yes. Not only did murdering the women make it so that there wasn't a chain, but also, the correct order of events must be played out. It's why Caelin couldn't kill his father, why the order of the jewelry needed to be correct, and that some people, sadly, had to die. Those men chasing you, and the ones that are still on their way here, they have parts to play, even as we do to make this happen."

"Are we close?" She nodded at Lewis. "And from what I understand, no one has gotten this far before, have they?"

"No. None of the other families have been able to get any more than three of the women to their hearts. While children were born of them, to complete the next generations, there wasn't enough magic for it to be completed."

There was more she could tell them, about the young miss coming, how she was to be treated on her way, and what she was doing to get here. She could also tell them that even now the castle was beginning to repair itself, that the walls surrounding it were being fortified so that when they went there, and they would, it would be strong enough to hold them all safely within her belly.

"And this sword, why did I get it and not the others? Not Kenton, or even someone that would be here all the time to use it should Butler come here." She could almost feel sorry for Vance. He was the strongest of them all, but also the weakest. His heart wasn't as theirs, nor was it ready for his mate. But he would find a way to let her in, or she'd make him. Laughing a little, she answered him as best she could.

"No one has the power to make it useful but you, Vance. Not because you are a warrior of heart, nor because you have seen more death and witnessed more horror than all of them together. You have it because the sword knew that you could do it. You would need it to end this horrific time in all our lives." He didn't seem to be convinced...she could almost feel it rolling off him. "You will understand more when the time comes for you to do so. And in answer to your question about Butler, he is here now. Not in this town, but close by. He is done with the peons, as he calls them, not doing what he needs. He will come for us all himself."

"But you have the last piece." She nodded at Kenton. "Does she know that? The woman coming, does she know that you have it?"

"She doesn't know anything about any of you. Nor is the dragon capable of helping her. She will arrive, and I've been told she is on her way. But for her own safety, I think she will do better than any of us did because she knows nothing. They cannot find her if she doesn't have the magic from the jewelry that we have surrounding us."

~~~

Lewis closed and locked the door after his family left. He'd started dinner while they were there, inviting them to join them. But they declined, saying that they needed to get to their own homes and to think. He could understand that. When he entered the kitchen, Raven was there talking with Poe.

"I do not understand why you think it important that I stay in this part of the house. You have given me vague answers as well as half-truths. If you don't wish me to be around, I can go out of doors and stay in the big barn." He didn't have a barn, big or small. But Poe continued before she could answer. "What is it you're really doing here?"

"I want to have sex." Poe said nothing, but Lewis thought he got it then. "With you about, I will not be relaxed. I wish to bond with my mate, and with you about.... You will be squawking and making noises that will make me feel like you are telling me what I've done wrong. I would just as soon you were nowhere near me when I do this."

"I would never presume to do such a thing, but I understand that you don't wish me in the room with you. I could give you pointers. I have seen humans mate before. Disgusting, if you ask me, but I can tell you —"

"You will not, or I shall boil you in my pot the next time I need a raven claw." Poe leaped back from her and noticed him. When he said hello, Raven turned a nice shade of pink. "I was just talking to Poe."

"So I heard. Poe, where did you see a barn on the property? I don't think I've seen anything like that." He explained it to him. "So you made one? Whatever for? Not that I'm upset, but I would like to be asked about such things. Simply because I might have had plans for one myself."

"I checked, and you did not. But my lady here, Raven, needs a place to dry her herbs and to make her potions. I thought of just a small shed, but then I realized that I'd need a place to live. Also, there are other creatures that might enjoy staying out of the sight of humans, and a warm dry bed." He asked him what sort of other creatures. "The dragons, for one. There are two

62

here now besides the ones that the couple hold. They're small, yes, but there is a larger one coming too. Not overly large, but big enough to draw attention to himself should he be out and about. Also, there are creatures that Raven has at home. Ones that are no longer a part of your world. They'll come too, should you allow it."

"Why wouldn't I allow it?" He looked at Raven when Poe did. "Would you like to bring all the creatures and other things to this house? I'd be happy to make the arrangements to have them brought here for you."

"They're not what you would call conventional. I have my herbs, as Poe said, but there are other things as well. My mother's blankets that she made me. And I have a pair of goats and donkeys. There is a unicorn as well that roams the grounds where I lived, but I would have to ask her if she would like to come here. Would you tell me how this tastes? I cannot tell anymore." He took a sip of the broth that she held on a spoon and told her it was delicious. "Good. Also, you should know that I won't disturb you in your work if I have a place to call my own, and a garden."

"You may have anything and everything you wish." She turned to him, but he could tell that she wasn't ready to believe him yet. "I've never thought of donkeys and goats around here, but we can have a paddock put in for them. Unless they like to roam...then I'll talk to the pack about them too. A unicorn? I don't know what they'd want in the way of housing, but we can figure it out. As for you having a garden, I was working on putting one in anyway, a kitchen garden that I can use here as well as at the restaurant. Whatever you want, I promise you, we'll figure out a way to make it work."

"What if I told you that I'd like to have a large brewing pot put in the front yard? That I wanted to dance naked in the moonlight? Or that I wanted to butcher a child for my spells?" She was angry, and he wasn't sure why. Poe left them then, not a word spoken, but just left. "I'm not sure this will work."

"Shall we start at the beginning? I thought we were getting along nicely." She asked him how long he'd been standing there before Poe saw him. "Long enough to know that you don't want him around and why."

"I shouldn't have said that." He asked her why not. "I'm not a maiden, but I've not a lot of experience with sex. I thought it would be nice. A good thing for us to do."

"Yes, I think it would be as well." She told him not to make fun of her. Pulling her into his arms, he held her until she relaxed a bit. "I don't want you to rush into anything you don't want. I do want to make love with you, but I'm not going to make you, nor do I want you to do something that you're not fully committed to. All right?"

"I'm afraid that I will disappoint you. You are very nice, and I'm not used to your family either. They're very loud, aren't they?" He said that they were, and thanked her for telling him he was nice. "Would you like to have sex with me?"

"No." She stiffened, and he held her when she started to pull away. "I wish to make love with you. There is a difference, and I would gladly love to show you."

"You're making fun of me." He assured her that he was not. "I don't understand you. When I first came here, all I wanted to do was to live out my days with you and not bother you at all.

64

Beg you for a garden and a place to call my own. A place that I could hide from you should I need to. But you have been more than generous, as well as kind to us. Even accepting of Poe. What sort of person does that with a stranger?"

"A man who would like to show his mate that he is a kind man, and generous. A man that can make room for a raven in his home, as well as a garden and a place for you to call your own. Why? Because I want you to be happy. I want you to be able to be yourself around me. To know that above all else, I will love you, care for you, and to try my best not to chase you around your pot that you threatened poor Poe with, and see what you make when you do." She laughed. It was something that, while she had giggled a little, seemed to be rusty to her. Vowing to make sure he made her laugh every day, he leaned down to her. "May I kiss you, Raven? To see if you taste nearly as good as I think you will? To feel you open beneath me, to know what it's like to kiss someone that I have fallen deeply in love with."

"Yes. But...." He pulled back and frowned. "I'm starving. I mean, like I've not eaten for a week, and my belly thinks I've been cut off. All the smells coming from the oven? They're making me hungrier than I think I've ever been before."

Laughing again, he pushed her to the table and told her to sit. He'd put all the dinner in one pan so that they'd be able to eat easily. The roast was tender as he put it on the platter. And when he put the potatoes and carrots all around it too, he thought of the taste she'd given him.

"You made the gravy. I love it. And I have fresh bread too. I don't normally use a bread maker, but today, with all this going on, I thought it would be quicker." While he decanted everything else, she set the table. She was getting around the kitchen like she had been doing it all her life, and it made him feel better about her being here. Not that he wasn't thrilled to death anyway, but if he had to leave her, she'd be all right by herself. As soon as they were seated, he got up to get her a drink. "I have tea, but it's not sweet; is that okay?"

"I can fix that." He watched as she touched the side of the glass and the liquid in it swirled around. Living with a witch was going to take some getting used to, he thought.

Dinner was fun. They talked about everything but nothing too serious. She told him of the things that she had at her home, a small place that opened into the mountain behind her, and he told her how he'd come to have this house. By the time he was serving her ice cream over cookies, and he had a piece of apple pie, they were about as comfortable with each other as he'd ever been around another person.

When she yawned three times in as many minutes, he asked her to join him in going to bed. She wasn't timid about it, and he was nervous. Whether or not they made love, he wanted her to be beside him. Opening the bedroom door, he asked her if he could join her. Her smile was bright enough to light up the world, he thought.

"I was wrong about you, Lewis. You're more than kind and generous. I think you're the sweetest person that I've ever met. Thank you for this day in getting to know you. And your family. I'd be honored if you came to bed with me." He kissed her then, put all that he had in the kiss so that she'd know that he was already in love with her. "I love you too. More than I ever dreamed possible when I started out on this journey to come to be your mate."

"I love you too." He held her to him as he closed the door behind him. "But I have to tell you, if Poe even tries to come into this room tonight, you won't have to boil him in your pot. I'll pluck every one of his feathers out and make him eat them. Right before I shove him in the closet."

She was laughing when he lifted her up in his arms. Lewis was going to do this right. And starting right at this moment, he was going to make sure that she had everything and anything she wanted. Lewis didn't care what it cost him either, she was going to make him happy with her own happiness.

"I want to see you." She nodded. "Then when I have you naked, I'm going to taste every single inch of you, starting with your lovely breasts."

"Yes, I'd like that very much." He growled low in his throat when she touched her hand to his cock. "Then when you have had your fill, I plan to do the same to you."

Yes, he thought, she could have anything and everything she wanted. Starting with him. Lewis was in love, and didn't care who knew it.

Chapter 5

Raven loved the way that he touched her. Her skin felt silky one moment and hard as stone the next. And when she was tensed up, he would only need to slide his tongue over her. That would be all it took to make her explode with a quick release, but it was never enough.

"Lewis, you're killing me." He laughed, and she wanted to scream at him to give her what she wanted. Not that she had any idea what it was, but he was holding back something, and she wanted it in the worst sort of way. Then he moved down her body, nipping and licking a path from her breasts to her navel.

She'd never been very proud of her body, not that she had seen it in a great many years. She knew that she had all the parts to make a man want her, but was not really sure if it was enough. Or in her case, too much.

Her breasts were large, more than she could easily fit in

both her hands. Her nipples were large too, as if they'd been suckled a great deal and they'd been stretched. But Lewis seemed to like them. He had laved them with his touch, pulled them with his fingers, and made her crazy with his mouth. But what he was doing to her belly button was making her pussy feel wet and hot.

"You smell so good." Nodding, she held her breath as he held himself over her apex. "I cannot wait to taste you here. To have you coming down my throat. To feel you tightening around me. Christ, I love you."

If he expected her to say something back, she wasn't able to manage it. Her scream of release took her breath away and nearly strangled her with the need to come again. Lewis suckled at her nubbin, the part of her she rarely thought about, until she came four times, hard. And when he slid his fingers into her sheath, she came again and again, until her body felt like one of her wet towels that she'd tossed over the line on laundry day.

"You need to stop." He didn't, of course, but continued his exploration of her body. Every time she thought he might be close to stopping, lifting his head away from her, he would begin anew, and she'd scream again when he brought her over.

Finally, when he moved up her body again, still tasting and licking her, she cried out when he took her nipple into his mouth and bit down. Christ, if she came one more time, she was going to die. There would be no dragon because she would have been killed by sex.

"I want to fill you." Her body took on more energy then, seemed to be ready for whatever he wanted to give her now. As he held his cock at her entrance, she could feel how thick it was, how hard and full he was as well. "I need you."

"Yes, please." He filled her. Raven cried out with another release and grabbed onto his shoulders for what he was doing to her now. As he pounded her hard, she wanted more, needed more as he licked along her throat. She wanted to feel him come inside of her, to feel him making her his own. And when he bit down on her throat, she did the same to his shoulder and screamed around the flesh. As soon as he came, his hot cum marking her in a way that she'd never dreamed of before, she came again, this time fainting from the sheer pleasure of it.

When she woke, she was laying over him, his hands moving up and down her back. His cock was still hard and deep within her, so when she lifted her head up to kiss him, she felt it stretch inside of her. Then, before she could follow through on her plan, she found herself on her back and knew that his face was close to her own.

"Did I hurt you?" Shaking her head, she told him never. "Good. When you fainted on me, I thought for sure that I'd broken you. I never was very good at keeping my toys in one piece."

She had no idea why she thought that was funny, but he kissed her on the nose as he filled her over and over again. Wrapping her legs over his pushed him deeper inside of her, filled her in a way that he'd not done before. And when he lifted her ass up, bringing her body closer to his, she could feel her nubbin touching him harder and longer, and it brought her again.

This time when she opened her eyes, she was alone in the big bed. Moving to feel around the room, she realized how

71

sore she was and had to smile. Raven hadn't thought of the workout she'd get from just having sex. She made her way to the bathroom to take a shower. Not knowing the time except by the warmth of the sun coming through the window on her face, she thought it was well after noon.

It took her a couple of tries to find herself something to wear. Her clothing hadn't been moved in here yet, and she had no idea where her things were. So going to his dresser, she found socks and a pair of his briefs, as well as a T-shirt. Her bra she found on the floor, nearly tripping over it, but the rest was nowhere to be found.

Going down the stairs carefully, she followed her nose to the kitchen. She could hear him speaking, and wondered if she was covered enough to enter the room if he had company. But when he paused, presumably to let someone speak, she thought he was on the phone talking. Poe joined her in the big hall before she could go into the kitchen.

"He let me in this morning. I nearly told him that he didn't have to, that I could let myself in, but it was so nice of him that I couldn't find it in my heart to disappoint him." She told him he was a good man. "He is. By the way, your clothing has been shipped here. Caelin took care that you had some of your things too. They are in the garage."

"I'll have to thank him." Poe moved off her shoulder as she entered the kitchen. Lewis was cooking, she knew that, but what it was she didn't know. But when he kissed her on the mouth and told her to have a seat, she wasn't sure if he was off the phone or not until he spoke again.

"Yes, I'm sure that I want you to go and serve him this time.

72

Having him lurking about the building might get him hurt or killed. This way, if he's there and gets hurt by one of the wolves, then it's all on him." He paused again, then laughed. "All right then. I'll go there today. Thanks for helping me with this."

When he sat down at the table with her, he reached over and took her hand into his. There wasn't any need for him to explain to her what he had been doing, but he did anyway. Before she could forget again what she'd found out when she touched Byron, she told him.

"There is something in the building. Money or trunks. His mind was too hyped up for me to get exactly what it was." Lewis asked her if she wanted tea, and when she said yes, he told her where it was when he finished it. "He thinks that whatever is down there is worth the risk of taking me and holding me for ransom until you sign the building over. My goodness, this is very good."

"It's breakfast casserole. I had some left over from when Gavin was here yesterday. I just added some gravy to it. The police said I should go there today and have a look around. To see if he's taken anything, or what reason he'd have to risk pissing me off to get it." She told him that he'd been in the building several times. That what he wanted was in the back of it. "You want to go with me when I look? Oh, before I forget, I got a package for you. I didn't get it, but it turned up in the garage. It doesn't have a name on it, but I think you know who might have sent it."

"Yes, Caelin did. It has some of my things in it." He told her that it wasn't very large. "Well, it wouldn't have to be, not really. I think he might have used some magic to get a great

73

deal more in it than it appears."

"Well, you put it wherever you wish. And I've had a look at the barn. I don't know why, but I expected it to be about the size of a nice sized shed. It had three levels, as well as stalls full and ready for whatever animals that we want to put in it. So, you should make whatever arrangements you want for those too." She heard him pick up some paper, and he told her that he had a list of things too. "I have to go by the bank, with you. You need to sign a few forms for our money to be used. Also, I've had your name put on the deed here, as well as all the other properties that I own. You now have what I have. And when you're ready, we can get you more things to wear when we get done with the building. If you still want to go with me. Then I have the rest of the afternoon to prepare for the wedding tomorrow afternoon."

"You have a busy day. I will need someone to help me with my money as well. Can you recommend someone?" He told her that the banker they were going to was trustworthy. "All right. I do need clothing, but I also need you to show me where you put them when you remove them from me. I couldn't find them this morning."

"That was the plan, my dear." He kissed her on the mouth. "I washed them. I've been up for a while and I threw them in with mine. I hope you don't mind."

The man was just too nice for words. When he handed her the clothing, she pulled them to her nose. They smelled of his things, fresh and warm still. Going into the small bathroom to change, she wondered what he'd do if she told him of all the things that might be coming their way. Money that she had, as well as not just a unicorn, the likes of which humans hadn't seen before, but she also had a griffon, and a friend of hers was a troll. Giggling, she pulled on her clothing and thought one thing at a time right now. They had to take care of Butler, and the new bride coming, as well as the things in the barn. Today, she thought, was going to be the first happy day of her life.

The ride to town was informative. The box in the barn was left for later; Poe told her that it would be all right. Lewis pointed out places for her. Not that she'd be able to find them on her own right away, but she did know now that there was a beauty parlor that served mostly the town's elderly, and that they only, as far as he could see, had one hair style, and she was much too young for that.

There was the bakery that Emma owned, as well as the antique shop that Jasmine and her son ran. They were very good at flipping things they picked up at auctions or tag sales, so if she had some things to get rid of, they could do it. He told her where Kenton and Gabe's offices were in the event that she needed them, as well as where his restaurant was near those places.

"The wedding is tomorrow. And I think, knowing my mom, she's pulled a few strings for us to be married at the same time. Or pretty close to it. Would you mind?" She asked him if he did. "No. I mean, I thought I would, but no, I'd love to be married to you. And I'll do it properly as soon as I find the perfect ring for you."

Overwhelmed in that moment, she felt the need to run. Telling him to stop the truck, she reached out beyond anything anyone could see and felt what was there. She knew that magic was close, but what sort, she hadn't any idea.

"Where is the shifter?" He told her that it was in his freezer at the restaurant. "Good. I'll deal with it first, but something is out there. Not close…I mean, not where I can see what it is with my magic, but it's out there."

"Do we need to get back to the house? I don't want anything to happen to you." She told him she was fine, as were the rest of them, but they had to be careful. "Always. And now that we have a heads up, I should tell you that I can smell evilness. I haven't any idea if that'll be useful or not, but that's what I smelled when the shifter came pretending to be you."

"I can as well. It's a little harder for me, simply because I have both kinds of magic, but knowing that you can, that'll help. I'll teach you the different kinds of smells for each kind of magic too." When she told him to go on, Raven called Poe to her. As soon as they stopped, he was waiting for her. "I think something is out there. Would you have a look? But be very careful, please. I don't want whatever it is to know what you are."

Once they were in the bank she felt better. The man that ran this place was trustworthy, and she liked him. He was very helpful too with the paperwork, because he had a sister that had been blind from birth. After all the paperwork was signed and arrangements were made concerning her money, they walked to the restaurant. Time to take care of the shifter.

~~~

Emma was in the big kitchen when Lewis and Raven arrived. She'd been putting the pieces of cake in the walk-in, so it would be ready to assemble tomorrow. When the large pickle jar was brought out of the cold storage, she asked if she could watch whatever was going to happen.

"Of course. You might not care for my methods, but it needs to be dealt with." Emma said that however she got rid of the thing was fine by her. "Good. First thing, however, I need to speak to it. And Butler will hear me. He won't know where we are, only that I'm talking to his creation."

"Will he be able to hurt you from wherever he is?" Raven told Lewis that he couldn't. "Good. I don't want anything to happen to any of us, not with things so close, but the fact that he sent that thing here to kill me...well, I want it gone as well."

The jar was set on the counter and Raven called to it. The creature moved around the jar several times before it paused in front of her. Emma stayed back out of the way, but she could see that the magic of the thing was as black as day old coffee.

"Who sent you here? And why?" The shifter answered her, saying that King Butler had done so to kill one of the McCade men. "He is no longer king. The castle that he was a part of is no longer his to command. I do."

"You are a witch, the one that he wishes to take to his bed." Emma thought that wasn't right, but the shifter spoke again. "He wishes to kill you as he fucks the life out of you, as he did your mother."

"My mother was beheaded, not like he says." The shifter stirred around in the jar, then settled again. "You have checked? You know what I say is true?"

"Yes, he lied." Raven said that he was very good at that. "He wishes for me to kill your mate or the other man and take the jewels."

"The jewels are a part of our bodies. You cannot take them without killing the host." The shifter stirred again. "You cannot kill what does not harm you or your master."

"He wishes them dead?" Emma moved closer, but not enough to touch the thing. But it looked directly at her. "You are magical, and hold the dragon's heart that protects you all. You are very powerful. I cannot kill you."

"You can't kill any of us." The shifter looked at Raven. "She is going to destroy you because you were told to come here. You can't kill any of us."

"I was to kill the male before he found his mate. He knew some about her, and I knew some that King Butler told me. That was going to make him trust me. But he did not." No one spoke as the shifter worked things out on its own. "Power is very strong in this room. Are you going to destroy me, Raven of the mountain?"

"Yes. I am." Raven put her finger on the metal lid and Emma saw it heat up. When it was hot, so hot that it was white with it, the shifter moved to the bottom of the jar, trying to stay as far from the heat as it could. "You will be no more."

The jar exploded, but glass didn't fly around as she thought it would have. Instead, it lay on the counter like it had been laid there after it was broken. The shifter, and its dark magic, was gone, not even a poof of smoke to say that it had ever been.

"Cover your ears." The urgency of Raven's voice had her doing what she said. Even with her fingers deep in her ears, Emma could hear the scream of something, like an animal in a great deal of pain. Then, just as it had started, it ended too. The shifter was gone, as well as the glass that had held it inside. "I'm sorry. I should have warned you sooner. Are you all right?"

Nodding, she sat down on the floor. "That was...I have no idea. But that was painful. I cannot imagine what it would have sounded like had you not had me cover my ears. Is that thing dead?"

"Sort of." There was more. Emma didn't know why she felt that, but she knew there was more. So when she asked her, Raven told her. "The maker, Butler, is going to be in a great deal of pain once the shifter finds him. And that won't be too hard to do, since Butler is making no bones about hiding out."

Emma laughed. It was funny really the way that Raven got back at him. It wasn't big things, but things that even she thought of as fantastic. If she had hung out with criminals, as Emma had done, then there would have been no stopping the kind of mayhem that she might have caused.

Chapter 6

The package was magical, and every time she reached into it to pull something else out, Lewis was astounded. Item after item came out. A goat, as well as two donkeys. When the second goat came out, he didn't even try to look like he wasn't surprised. The little guy came and sat right on his lap as the magic wore off him and he grew to his normal size.

In addition to the animals, she had several large handmade blankets. A handwoven basket full of herbs and other plants. Lewis laughed when she pulled out a miniature dresser, as well as a chair. But almost as soon as she shook them a bit and put them down, they started to grow as well.

"You have to admit, it would be a nice way to travel if you wanted no one to know that you were moving out." She grinned at him, and he fell in love with Raven all over. "Is this all of it? I mean, the unicorn, will she be joining us here too?"

"Caelin said that she was thinking it over, but she didn't

want to travel in a box. I might have to go and get her." Lewis nodded when the goat took off to chase his sister. "There are a few more items in here as well. Would it freak you out if I just shook the bag to get them?"

"Is it dangerous?" Raven assured him that it wasn't. "Then shake away. Also, I have to get some feed for these little guys. And whatever the unicorn would eat. I never thought I'd have to say that either."

The bag that was inside the box was turned upside down. Another hard shake and a rocker tumbled out, as well as several knives and a table. When she picked up the table, setting it to the side, he thought that one was staying in the barn as it looked well-worn and smelled of several herbs at once. Then the large pot, cast iron he'd bet, came rolling toward him. Setting it upright, he watched as several items that he had no name for came out. She told him one was a drying rack, much like people used for socks in the winter, as well as a small box of photos and another rocker.

"I'd like to put these on the deck, if you don't mind." She asked him why he'd want to do that. Getting up, he sat down in one and moaned. "They're much more comfortable than they look, too. Yes, on the deck. I can see the two of us out there, rocking away the evening while sipping on some tea."

"Brew." He corrected himself. "What time do you have to be at the restaurant in the morning? It's the big day, right?"

"Yes. The cake isn't put together yet. Emma said she'd do that tomorrow, so it would be fresh. I've not seen it, but she said it's her greatest masterpiece to date." The rest of the items were put into baskets and totes that had been brought out when they came to see what Caelin had sent. "Everything is ready on my end, with the exception of cooking a few things. There isn't that much. The tables are set up. Plates are scattered around. And thanks to your help, nothing will be that difficult to clean up either. Thank you for suggesting to them about the heavy-duty paper plates."

"They're biodegradable as well, so that won't hurt the landfill. What do you think about putting this table in the greenhouse?" He hadn't known he had a greenhouse as yet, and smiled at her. "Oh. I think that Poe did that. It was a gift from Caelin. He said that he might have a need for something later, and didn't want to wait for the correct season."

"You can have whatever you wish, my love. The fact that you can have it put up with only a thought, that's wonderful as well. And I noticed that you finished the bedroom closet. No one would believe that there is that much room in there until you open the door." She flushed brightly, and he grinned. "Why don't you come over here and let me hold you for a little bit? Then we'll head into town, go see that stupid building that has Clayton all hot and bothered, and have some dinner. After that, we'll come back here and I'll ravish you."

"How about you go ahead to the building, I take a long bath, and be naked and ready for you when you return? I'm sure you could feast on me, should you wish." He stretched out his legs and asked her if he could get started now. "No. I've been working in this barn all day, and I smell like a goat. So do you, as a matter of fact."

He left after making sure that she was ready for him now. Lewis wasn't sure who had gotten more out of him teasing her, him or Raven, but as he drove to the building in the merchant district, he asked Vance if he wanted to meet him there.

Sure. I'm in the area now. I have two things that I'm looking into. He asked his brother if he could help him out. *Not with this, no, but I do have another project you can work on for me. I have to be away for a few months. Then when I return, I'm settling down and becoming a cop for the locals. Not full time, I don't want to do that, but I'm thinking I can't do as bad a job as they're doing right now.*

That's wonderful. He started to ask him about the tags in his body, but he pulled in behind him in his truck. "You working on getting those things out of your body, Vance? Or do I want to know?"

He entered the building ahead of him, and Lewis didn't think he was going to answer. Vance was good at that. If he didn't think you should know something or he didn't think you'd understand his reasons for something he was doing, he'd just not answer. But as soon as the door closed behind them, he leaned against the wall and looked at him.

"I'm going to be in deep shit when I take them out. And I'm going to, right before I kill the men involved in doing this to me." Lewis asked him if he knew who the players were. "Yes, there's three men. Men that I thought I could trust. Hell, Lewis, I thought all of us could trust."

"The president." He nodded, but said nothing more. "Who else? I'm assuming that it's some people high up on the food chain and in his offices."

"Yes. One of them is the vice president. I don't know how involved he is in this, but his name is on the paperwork as well. Then there is the guy running the Secret Service for the president. He is all over this shit. And the worse part of it is, he acts like we're the best of buds. You know me well enough to know that I don't play well with others." Lewis asked him how he was going to cover his ass. "You're assuming that I want to."

"Yes. I do. You wouldn't do anything to hurt Mom, and you know as well as I do that it will if you're caught doing this." Vance nodded, but didn't look like a man who cared. "What are you going to do? I want to help. Please?"

"No. As much as I'd like to have you there with me, I can't bring you into this. Not with the shit that is going to hit the fan. And there is a lot of shit going to be slung around before I'm done. I have two people working for me on the inside. These two people stand to lose more than I will if this goes public, and it will, but they're in as deep as I am. Both of them are people that have been tagged too, though differently." Lewis asked him how. "If they fuck up, they're dead. Their devices are set to go off if they monkey around where they're not supposed to. Mine are older, and that friend of Emma's, he said he can fix theirs to not go off, but he needs for them to trust him. That's not happening."

"Do you trust him?" Vance said that he trusted him with his life. "I've never heard you say that before. I'm assuming that the two of you, you've come to an understanding about this?"

"Yes. When I go dark, in the two months that I'm gone, he goes too. Not with me, but he'll be well cared for and hidden." Lewis asked when this was going to go down. "Soon. That's all I can tell you for now. When I leave here, the best I can do is tell you that I'm leaving. And if you don't hear from me, then

85

assume that I'm dead or so deep I can't connect with you."

"All right. I know that it has to be done, but I will worry about you." He nodded. "Okay, let's have a look in this building to see what dumbass is foaming at the mouth for. Raven said she thought it was something about money and trunks or trucks, but she can't get his mind to calm enough to know."

"I have to tell you, having a witch in the family is paying off." He asked him why as they moved through the upper levels. "The other day I came by your place and Raven was in the yard. I haven't any idea what she was doing besides planting something. Anyway, she made me promise that I wouldn't go to the bank that morning. I hadn't realized that I was going, but I told her I'd not. Then about an hour later, Mom calls and asks me if I could meet her down at the bank. I told her what Raven had told me, so we both didn't go. You know what happened? A woman came in, shot three people in the bank, then herself. Her house was ready to be foreclosed on, and she was upset."

"You think you might have been shot?" Vance just shrugged. "Well, I'm glad to know that someone is watching out for you. Maybe it would help you to have her touch one of those devices in your body. Perhaps she can tell you the outcome and warn you about getting hurt."

"I might." They covered both of the upper levels and made their way to the main floor again. "Not much here, is there? I mean, a lot of rat shit and dust, but nothing to get your panties in a knot about."

"I don't know either. Maybe he really does want it for sentimental reasons. Some people can be attached to the stupidest shit." They made their way to the basement and paused on the steps. "It looks like someone just took all the crap on the upper levels and brought it down here to dump. This will take a hell of a crew to clean up."

"Lewis, come here." Vance had walked ahead of him, and around the furnace that obviously wasn't working. There were four trunks there, and one of them had been left open. "That's a lot of green."

The money, in stacks around the trunk as well as inside of it, was wrapped in homemade wrappers. Each of them had been initialed, and a number was on the front of them that said the amount. Lewis picked up the first three stacks and quickly put them back. Those had added up to nearly ten grand.

Vance pulled a long blade from his boot and opened the other trunks. There was stacked up money in them as well. One of them had fifties, the other three had tens, twenties, and a mixture of everything respectively. Christ, there might well be over ten million in them all together.

"We have to make sure this isn't from a robbery or something." Vance only nodded and stared at the place beyond the trunks. "Are you listening to me, Vance? We have to call the police. This could be money from something big."

"I'm thinking that he might have been in on whatever it was." He asked him who he was talking about, and Vance pointed. "I think, in my opinion, that man has been dead for a decade or more. Probably killed about this money. Yeah, I'd call the cops, but I have to get out of here. You know that."

"Yes, I do." He didn't know what to do, and was relieved when Vance said he'd contacted Dalton. "What did you tell him? That there's a body and money, or you letting him walk into this as blind as we did?"

"I told him. You might want to remember what you touched while you were looking around. The money for sure, but neither of us got close to the body." Lewis watched his brother as he faded into the darkness of the room. "Also, call your mate. Unless you can do that funky thing she can do. Maybe you can figure this out before Dalton gets here."

"Right. I'm going to touch a dead man and see if I can figure out what killed him and why." Vance said it was worth a try. "I'll wait on Dalton, if it's all the same to you. If this doesn't work for me, then he'll know just what I touched. Christ, no wonder he wanted this building. No matter what he paid me for it, he still would have.... Do you think he saw the body?"

"Doubtful. The only reason I saw it was because I was looking for one. Don't know why, but I figured that something bad had to have gone down here." He looked around, then back at his brother. "You might be the luckiest bastard alive, or not, but had you sold him this building, no one would have found that body. Clayton would have made sure of it."

When Dalton showed up, he wasn't alone. Not only did he have Kenton with him to look at the body, but a second man who was using a camera. He started to tell them that Vance needed to leave when he realized that he was already gone. Like a fart in the wind, as his granddad used to say.

~~~

Kenton hadn't seen a body like this since his college days. It was mummified. Not only that, but someone had gone to the trouble of putting lye all around it and over it to hide the smell. He was sure that at some point there would have been a strong one, too. He looked around as the body was being photographed, and wondered what else they'd find down here. The place was a mess.

"The money will have to be processed. It might take as long as a few months to figure out if it's part of a robbery or not." Dalton asked Kenton if he'd heard of anything like that. "Not necessarily a robbery, but anything where a large sum of money was taken?"

"Nothing that I can think of, but then I was gone to college for a while. Mom might have an idea, but I don't know." Dalton said he'd ask her. Kenton turned to Lewis. "Have you touched it? I mean, to find out clues?"

They all knew that Raven could touch something and get a kind of reading from it, but they didn't know if Lewis could. It was as good as any time to figure it out, he thought. But when the large raven came into the room and landed on Lewis's shoulder, he looked at the bird too when it started to squawk. It occurred to him that the cop holding the camera might not take it so well if Poe did speak.

"I guess I can do it as well." Kenton nodded and watched his brother. "I don't know if I want to touch the man or not, but I can start with the money. Poe said that I had to think about it, not just touch it. I have to figure that out."

Lewis went to the first trunk and picked up one of the stacks. There was plenty of them to choose from, it seemed, but he took one off the trunk that Vance had opened. He said it might hold more information than the ones that they touched. Kenton thought that was a good point.

The basement was filled with crap, as they had said, but

there was a sort of flow to it. He stood up while his brothers did their thing and looked harder at the scene. The trash, it wasn't really trash but newspapers, and all of them were tied off except for one stack. Then there were the boxes of books.

Careful of what he touched, Kenton picked a random book out of a box. The title on the jacket of it was *Roundoff*, but the book itself was something different. A child's primer. The rest of the books in the box were the same. A dust jacket of one title, the book something a child would read. Then he looked at the bags of trash.

There was something off about those as well. Going to them, asking the cop that was using the camera for the station to go with him, Kenton pulled the first one away from the wall. Behind it was more newspapers, these tied off with a dark string. Just as he was reaching for the stack, he heard from Raven.

Don't touch it. Kenton jerked his hand back so quickly that he nearly hit the camera man. *Have your brother do it. And tell him to be careful. I think the murder weapon is close, or even in the bag.*

Since he'd not been able to tell what the man had died from, he wasn't sure how she would know, but then, the things that they could do now over just a year ago was a great deal. So, while Lewis held the money in his hand, Kenton called Dalton over and explained to him what he'd seen, as well as what Raven had told him.

"This is some messed up shit, Kenton. I'm just a cook. Not a murderer investigator anymore. But this, I think this was well above my paygrade even when I was." Kenton asked him what he wanted to do. "I'm not sure. I mean, Vance said this wasn't a big deal, and I believe that he would have the best handle on this, but shit, this is a murder that is older than all the years I have been out of college."

"I can tell you more when the body is moved, but Raven said that the murder weapon is there. It would go a long way in telling me a lot of things that might help. Not to mention, Clayton. What is his part in this? Just the money? Did he see the body?" Dalton told him if he did then he was in deep trouble too. "Because of what?"

"Hindering a police investigation. Messing with a known crime scene. Not reporting a crime. There is a list a mile long that he messed up on." Kenton couldn't help it, he laughed. "What the fuck is so funny about that?"

"He wanted the money. The building was only secondary. And now that you know why and what he did, he's never going to bother us again." When Dalton laughed, he felt better too. "The things people will do for some cash."

"Guys? I think I might have something here." They both moved to where Lewis was. He looked pale. "The guy didn't rob anything. Nor will you find that this money came from any kind of crime. He hoarded it from his family, including his parents when they passed away. Every time the business would have a good day, he'd bring the extra down here, hide it away in the trunks, then seal it up. He did that without his wife or anyone else knowing. And it got him killed."

"Do you know who did it?" Lewis nodded at Dalton, but didn't say anything more. "Lewis, I'm having a really shitty day, and I still have to go back and bake biscuits today, as well as a cherry cobbler. Tell me before I have to pistol whip you."

"You'd do that?" Dalton shook his head at Kenton. "Good. I mean, I can stitch him up, but I'd be more afraid of Raven should you hurt him. She's scary."

"He was murdered by his wife. She came down here, thinking the man was having an affair, and he was with all this cash. When he explained to her it was for them, she stabbed him in the throat. The reason is, the power at their house had been turned off and their child had gotten sick, and was even then in the hospital. Sadly, the wife took her own life too when her little girl passed away." Lewis looked at the trunks of money. "Greed. He had no reason to hoard this money, only that he was greedy. And now he's dead, his family is gone, and here it still sits with no one the wiser, and still in the trunks."

"Lewis, what do you want to do with this? The money is rightfully yours. The murder won't be solved, not by any means that we can prosecute anyone. And even if there was someone around that might want to cash in on this, you know as well as I do that there will people coming out of the woodwork on this." They both looked at the man holding the camera on them. "Don't worry about him. Your wife, she said that we could talk. The camera is off, and the film has been erased. It's better for everyone that way."

"We just bury him, put him in an unmarked grave and be done with it?" Lewis looked at Kenton. "Can you get on board with this?"

"Yes. I mean, so long as you don't do the same with the money. I think it could go a long way in helping out a lot of people. None of us need it. We could, I suppose, put it in the bank, but that would just raise more questions." He asked about

Clayton. "Sell him the building, but take out the body and the money, and sell him the building. It's no less than he deserves for what he's done."

Lewis looked around the place, then at him. He wasn't sure what he was thinking, but waited. Lewis was a thinker, a relaxed sort of one too. When he had something to work out, he usually just talked and talked until he was finished with it. But this time, Kenton had an idea that he was talking to Raven. Poe moved from his brother's shoulder to where the weapon was.

"All right. Raven said that we'll give him a proper burial and a headstone to mark his passing. The money we'll donate, in small amounts, to the local high school so kids can use it to go to college. To the shelter, as well as enlarging the clinic for the pack. Yes, I'm okay with this as well." Kenton was glad for it. "I've never used my dragon."

"You'll need to clean this place out after we get everything out of it. All right?" He nodded and looked at the trunks again. "What are you thinking?"

"Leave the trunks here. Take the money, of course, but leave them here once the place is cleaned out." Kenton laughed and so did Dalton. "I want him to think he's pulled one over on us. I mean, it's not like he can go talking about the missing money near a body, right?"

The guy with the camera just left them…laid it down on the floor and left. Kenton supposed that Raven had something to do with that, and when they heard the car start, Kenton picked up the camera that had been used and crushed it in his hands. Christ, this magic stuff was helpful.

Once they had the body removed, the pack coming in and

helping with that, they planned to have him put to rest on the back of their land. The money that they were going to donate to the pack was going to go a long way in helping them out, and they were glad to help.

Within two hours, much quicker than they thought it would work out, they had the entire basement cleaned out of anything to do with the murder, as well as the money. Raven showed up just as they were loading the last of the cash into the trucks. She told them what she'd done to help out.

"The young man that was here with you, he's gone home. He has a very bad cold, and won't be to work for a couple of days. No one seems to mind, as they don't have a lot of things going on right now. The camera and anything else he might have taken from the station are no longer on their books." Lewis thanked her. "I've also had the faeries find the dead man a nice spot on the land we were to use, and they're taking care of that."

"Lewis is going to clean up down here, then the trunks will be brought back in." Kenton looked around before continuing. "I can't wait to see Clayton's face when he figures out what has happened here today. No one will believe him, not after this is done. And if he makes a big stink of it, I might buy the building back from him for about half the price he paid."

He was still laughing as they exited the building. He and Dalton could have helped...they were used to their dragons, but Lewis was sure that he could control the burn so long as they were close by in the event that he had some issues. Kenton didn't think he'd have any trouble at all.

Chapter 7

Lewis wasn't entirely sold on this idea. It wasn't like they were covering up a murder that any of them had committed, but it still seemed wrong to him. Raven wrapped her arms around him and looked up at him. He smiled when she did.

"Do you know what will happen to this should the county or government be involved?" He nodded…he'd seen that too when he'd touched the money. "They'll put it in a box, one that will do nothing for the people here, and forget about it. Then after several years, someone will remember it and start to spend the money, on things for themselves. And no one, not even the man who takes it, will benefit from it. We can do that should you want, and I'll be behind you every step of the way, or we can help this town."

"You're making a good argument for the town." She kissed his chin. "I agree with you, on all of it. And getting Clayton in the end is something that I'm looking forward to. He should

95

have said something." She agreed with him. "I'm going to use my dragon to clean up. Until Kenton mentioned about burning away the evidence that might be here, I'd not thought about him once. And Warrior hasn't been as talkative either."

"I think that is Caelin's doing. He told him not to be so bothersome when it came to you guys. To keep you informed, but there is no reason for him to tell you every little thing he discovers about himself." Lewis told her that he sort of missed that about him. "Yes, well, you might take that back now that he knows."

I've missed you too, my lord. And should you ever find a need to speak to me, I am forever here for you. They both laughed. *Now, let us get this cleaned up. I have looked into the death of this man, and you should know, he was not a nice person. He would have his own family do without food and other needs when he had the funding to take care of them. Even going so far as to go to the food lines when they had more money than the agencies that put them out there.*

Lewis took a step back from Raven. Poe said that he would return—fire scared him—and Lewis let his dragon take him. It was and would forever be the scariest and most fun he'd ever had, he thought. When he noticed that his head bumped against the floor above him, he asked Raven if he was that much taller. She put her hands on his chest and moved them up to his shoulders.

"I would say that you are at least ten or so feet tall. I don't.... Wait, the blocks here. Let me count them." When she was finished, counting the block of walls as she moved her hands over them, he was almost afraid of her answer when she laughed. "You are nearly fourteen feet tall, and with your wings close to your body, you are about ten feet wide. I've not seen the others, but I think you to be bigger, from what I've heard. Also, I can almost see the information of your family's past. The women that had come before us, the men and how they died. I believe that was what the brooch was to bring you, the details of the past. My goodness, Lewis, it's been so long since I've touched a dragon. You are very handsome indeed, simply because you are my dragon."

He bowed before her and then looked around the room. The advice from Kenton was, start very small and work around the room. He wasn't sure how to start small when he didn't even know his own fire, but he opened his mouth to take in air. Letting out a small stream of fire from his nose felt odd but it didn't hurt, so he let a little more of it go.

You're doing very well, my lord. He thanked Warrior, and then asked him how he was going to put this fire out now that it was burning. *You only need to stomp on the smaller embers. Your feet are made for that, tough like they are.*

Once he was finished, the room only a darkened mass of soot, he, with the help of Raven, walked around the room and stomped out any embers that might catch. Kenton and Dalton did the same; their dragons were smaller than his, but not by much. He wondered at the difference until Warrior mentioned that he'd brought to them the knowledge of all the McCades before them, and it would take a day or so for them to receive it as well. The magic, apparently, made them larger each time. Not that the knowledge was to make them bigger, these memories, but they'd need their size to keep that safe as well. All in all, he thought it a good morning. But he had a great deal yet to do.

Bringing the trunks back in, setting them up in the room where they'd been, was easy enough. The garbage was all gone, the newspapers that they could preserve had been taken out to donate to the locale library to see if they wanted them. If not, then he thought that there were people in town that might enjoy reading them. Some of them were nearly seventy years old.

Just as they were ready to leave, Raven went to one of the trunks and dropped a penny inside. Saying nothing, she left the three of them there and Lewis laughed.

"He is going to be so pissed off. I think I might put in some cameras, so we can have a look at him when he finds out he's been had." Dalton said it was no less than he deserved, as he'd planned to do the same to Lewis. "Yes, but I'd have not known about it. He was fully aware of taking me to the cleaners, so to speak."

Going to the restaurant felt better to him. He did have a lot to do, but he felt lighter for it. And having Warrior to speak to felt like he'd been reunited with an old friend. They talked for hours while he got things ready. And by dinner time he was set. Not only were things on trays to put in the oven when the time came, but he had a menu sorted out for his grand opening as well. Simple was best, he'd thought, and his first night was going to be two things…chicken and beef.

Dropping the menu to be printed up, he walked to the diner to have dinner with Raven. Her day had been messed up by a couple more things than the building, and he decided that when he got her home, they were going to hit the hot tub then the bed. Making love to his wife all night was something that he was really looking forward to.

"Hello, Lewis. I see that you're about ready to open the Dragon's Lair. I bet that set you back a pretty penny." Clayton sat at the table next to them as he spoke. "I don't suppose you'd let me buy that building off of you now, would you? I mean, you could probably use the capital about now, I'm thinking?"

"If I sell you this building, will you leave me the fuck alone?" The greed on Clayton's face made him ill. Lewis had never liked the man, and he was sure that no one else in town did either. "I'm sorely sick to death of you coming to me every day about it. If I do this, will you shut the fuck up and never bother me again?"

"Deal. How much do you want for it? Now, I want you to know that I know how much you paid for it. And while the area is coming together, it's not at the end, where this place is. So, let's be fair about it." Lewis looked at Raven, and she nodded as if they had talked about a price. "You sell it to me for a good price and I'll never come to you again."

The burble of laugher startled him, but Lewis said nothing. The man was stupid if he thought this was going to be an easy sale for him. So, knowing what the man wanted out of it, and knowing too what he wasn't going to get, he named his price. Clayton put out his hand and asked if they could go to the bank today.

"I should go and see if there's anything in it that I might want, don't you think?" Clayton actually looked like he was going to hit him, but only shook his head. "Oh well, I guess if I haven't gone to find if there was anything in it by now, then I guess I didn't really want it. Okay, bank it is. I'll just make a call and see if Colin can come here. My wife and I have just ordered."

In less time than it took for their food to arrive, Colin came to their table with all the paperwork, as well as the deed to the building. Lewis was making a good deal of profit, even not counting the money they'd found. He'd only paid a buck for it ten years ago when the town was trying to spruce up the area. That, like a lot of projects, had gone by the wayside when they couldn't get anyone else but his family to purchase the buildings.

As soon as they signed the deed over and had it notarized, Lewis had a bad moment. He didn't know why, but as soon as it was there, it was gone again, so he let it go. While they ate their dinner, letting Colin and Clayton join them, all he could think about was now that this was done, he just wanted to take a nap, for about a month.

"I heard that your brother had a good show in Paris last month." Lewis told Colin that it had been fun for them all. "That woman that is in there with him, Harper, she sure is a hoot. Came into the bank the other day, and was sort of embarrassed to be putting that check she had in her account. I assured her that it was fine, that we dealt with Jorden too, and she gushed over him like he was some big star. When all the while, I was thinking how big a star she is."

"They are both in awe of the other. It's funny to see them together. They're like a couple of teenagers that have seen their first artist." Lewis related the story about a family dinner and how they were around each other. "I tell you, it was all we could do not to point out to them that they were both equally

100

famous, and to get over it."

After dinner and dessert, Clayton left. Lewis knew that he couldn't go into the building until tomorrow—the paperwork needed to be filed—but he was nearly dancing when he left them. Colin didn't say anything…he didn't have to. They all knew that Clayton was going to go there anyway. It was only a matter of time before he came around again. When Colin left them, with the assurances that he'd see them at the wedding tomorrow, Raven leaned against Lewis as they enjoyed some tea. Brew. They enjoyed some brew.

"Do you suppose this will end with him?" Lewis told her not until Clayton got himself in trouble over it. "Yes, you and I both know that he's going to get himself in deep over this."

"My mom can handle herself." They knew that as well, and why she would need to. "I won't warn her—I don't think that would help—but I would like for Poe to keep an eye on her for us. She's immortal, but she can still be hurt."

"I've sent him to her…he does like her. She'll know he's around, of course, but she won't know why. I agree with you, this is the best way to handle this." He and Raven made their way to his truck. He didn't know how she'd gotten into town, but she rode home with him. Magic, he supposed.

The hot tub seemed to call to him. Asking Raven to join him, they undressed in the house and made their way out to the deck. The night was cool, cooler than it had been in a while, and they sat on either side of the tub enjoying the night. When Raven moved to sit on his lap, he helped her slide over him. Having her this way was better than he could have imagined.

"The way you touch me…do you have any idea how that

makes me feel?" She moved her hips and he moaned as he held her. "Lewis, I want you to let me come like this. To ride you until I have my release."

"Honey, whatever you want, I'm here for you. But I don't know if I can just let you come without me joining you." She giggled, and he held her tighter. "You are so beautiful. I don't think I tell you that enough. Nor how much I love you."

She rode him slowly, her hips moving back and forth, her hands cupping her large breasts until he was mad with wanting her. When she offered him one, he took it greedily, suckling hard on the tip until she screamed out her release.

"Come for me again, love. I want to feel you tighten around me again and again." He held her tightly as he played with both of her breasts. They were tight and soft at the same time, and he couldn't seem to get enough of them. When she stood up he wanted to beg her to come back, but she leaned over the side of the tub and he stood up behind her.

"I'm going to come all over you like this." She reached between her legs and wrapped her hand around him. "Christ, love. I might not make it to bring you again if you keep that up."

"To feel you coming over me, that'll be enough to make me come again." Lewis fucked her hand, and when she moved, bracing herself on the tub, he entered her hard and fast. "Come with me, Lewis. I need it."

Lewis didn't want to disappoint her, so he fucked her hard, splashing water not only over the side but also all over them. The cool night and the hot water made for some erotic feelings, and when Raven slid her fingers into her pussy, curling around his cock, he came hard.

His body bowed back while his cock filled her. Lewis held onto her hips, knowing that he was going to leave a mark, but he didn't care. Raven was his, forever and ever, and he felt his cock and balls fill again as she cried out her own releases.

Leaning over her, filling his hands with her breasts, he tugged hard on her nipples, loving the way that she seemed to enjoy it. When she told him she was coming again, Lewis knew that this time he was going to make her faint. He so loved having her wake up from sex in his arms.

Cupping her breast in one hand, he slid his own fingers into her nether lips and found her hard nubbin. Squeezing it as hard as he thought she could stand, he was rewarded with cream filling his hand, her breast tightening so tightly in his hands that he wanted to suckle it. And when she screamed this time, her voice loud in the night air, an answering echo of a wolf sounded with her, and he knew that the world around them knew that he'd satisfied his mate tonight.

~~~

Byron was at the bank when the banker Colin showed up. He'd been waiting on the man for nearly an hour, and was trying his best not to push him into his seat before he was ready. As soon as he had his jacket off and was ready to start his day, Byron nearly jumped his desk to get him to file the paperwork.

"There's a problem." Byron was shaking his head as soon as Colin spoke. "I'm afraid there is. You need to sign a few more documents before you can claim the building. One is from the county. It says that now that the other buildings are being renovated, you must do the same in a timely fashion so as it's not an eyesore when the other businesses are up and running."

"How long do I have?" Not that it mattered to him. He was going to leave town as soon as he got the money. Byron hadn't even decided if he was going to pay the mortgage off or not yet. "I mean, are they going to expect me to, I don't know, have it done by the end of the month?"

"Oh no, you'll have the usual eighteen months to get some improvements done on it, then you'll have to have it completed within five years. And there are some stipulations on that as well." He pulled out a sheet of paper, and Byron asked him how long this was going to take. "I have to read it to you, Mr. Clayton, then you have to sign it saying that I read it to you. They're taking no chances that you aren't aware of the things that need to be done."

Byron sat there, listening to the man drone on about water and electricity. He had his own plans, and none of them included him doing any kind of repairs on the building, not even to replace the glass that he'd broken to get into the place. It was his, and the sooner he could go and claim it, the sooner he could get his ass out of town.

He'd wanted to go to his building last night, but he knew that since he'd been told he couldn't, not until things were filed, that he'd be arrested. Until things were done in the proper order, he didn't own the building just yet, and Byron didn't want to fuck this up when he was so close to the finish line.

When Colin looked at him, he realized that he should have been paying attention. As it was now, he had no idea what had been said to him or what he might have to agree with to get inside the place. Byron had purchased himself a new truck last week, just to haul away his money.

His money. Byron had done a lot of research about the money too. There hadn't been any robberies that he knew of that would account for the funds. And all he could find on the people that had owned it was a couple that had disappeared, though he knew where the man was, as well as a company about seventy years ago that had gone belly up when they'd tried to manufacture baskets, of all things.

"This next paper has to do with the loan that you're taking out. I don't like to tell clients what to do with such things, but are you sure that you wish to use your home as collateral, Mr. Clayton? As well as your pension? That is a great deal you're putting at risk. And if you don't do as you've said you would, in the other paperwork, then you'll be out of a great deal of ready money." Byron laughed; he couldn't help himself. And when it seemed as if it was getting out of control, he put his hand over his mouth to stop it. Colin just stared at him with a frown. "Are you all right?"

"Yes, fine. Just fine and dandy. Yes, I know it's a lot of money to put up for this place. And I'd not have had to if Lewis had come down in his pricing." Which had surprised him too. Lewis had taken his offer and didn't quibble at all. He wondered if he'd.... No, no, the man was much too busy to be going into the building, especially after all this time. "Had I known that he was going to take my first offer, I might have...well, that's water under the bridge now. I have it, and he does not. Now, I know this to be a fact, but the building, that would include all the contents too, correct? He can't come back on me, saying that he didn't know something was in there and want it now?"

"No, he even had me put that in the contract for you. He doesn't want anything that was in the building when he sold it to you. It's all yours. I'm to understand that he has owned it for a very long time. I wonder what made him sell it now." Byron told the man that he'd seen an opportunity and didn't let it go. "I suppose. Now, I'll just go now and file this for you, and as soon as I return, you can own it."

"If you don't mind, I'll go with you. I want to see it filed." Again he was looked at strangely, but he only smiled. "I have plans for the building, you see, and cannot wait to get started on them."

He didn't know what to do about the body. The man had been dead for a long time; of course, there wasn't any way that they could blame that on him. But he hadn't reported it. Nor had he asked for assistance with the man. He supposed that could get him into some trouble, but he wasn't going to hang around long enough for anyone to notice it. Byron Clayton was a man with a plan.

Of course there was a line. Not terribly long, but enough so that they were there for an extra hour. It might have gone faster had not Colin seemed to need to speak to every person that moved by them. Some of them were strangers just asking for directions. The man was driving him insane.

After things were filed in the proper place, he had to wait a little while longer while a copy was made for him. He wasn't sure that he might need it, but he wanted a copy in the event that the pack was still hanging around when he got there. Byron wanted nothing getting in his way when he got his cash.

While walking to his car, he made himself slow down. If he

had run, like he wanted to, then people might have taken note. He hadn't any idea why it mattered—he was washing the dirt of this town off his shoes as soon as he could—but no one was going to say that he'd done something wrong when they found out that he'd made a killing off this sale.

The buildings around his were being worked on when he arrived. Waiting a few moments to see if one of the workers was going to make a big deal of him being there, he thought he might well have been invisible for all the attention they paid to him. Byron got inside the building, using the key this time, and did a fast jig when the door was locked behind him. It was his. All his.

He surveyed the rest of the building first. He wanted to make sure that nothing had been disturbed. Byron wished now that he'd taken pictures of the place when he'd been there, just to be assured that nothing had been taken without his permission. Laughing again, he thought he needed to get more control over his life, or they were going to have him locked up before he could spend his first million. After looking through all the floors and finding nothing more than a sooty smell, he stood at the stairs that would take him to his treasure. And what a treasure it was too.

"I'm going to go away for a long time, and I'll buy whatever I wish, no matter the price." He leaned his forehead on the door and let out several breaths before he moved to open the door. "Get ahold of yourself, Byron. Or before you know it, you'll fall down the fucking stairs and break your fool neck. And the only people that will make anything from this gesture is the county coroner, and he won't even give you a proper burial."

107

Opening the door was easier than he thought it would be. The doors to the upper floors were stiff with not being opened for a long time. He'd only been up this way the one time, to make sure that there wasn't anything else that he could claim, and found it to be a dreary and dark place. Going down the stairs with his flashlight skimming over the walls, he noticed that there was soot there as well. Not that he would have noticed the other times he'd been there, so he dismissed it. As soon as he was at the bottom of the stairs, however, he knew that he'd been taken.

The place was cleaned up. The trash bags and stacks of paper were gone, as well as the body. Byron went up the stairs again to make sure he was in the right building, but knew what he saw there had been true. Lewis had found his money.

"No, no, no." He walked around the empty place several times. The trunks were still there, but he knew as surely as he was standing in a worthless building that he owned now that they were as empty as this place was. There wasn't going to be any leaving the country now. No buying him a fast boat. And he wasn't going to be able to make a fresh start someplace else. All the money that he'd had—the house, his pension—it was all gone now too. Just because Lewis McCade had tricked him. "He's messed with the wrong man, he has."

He walked to the first trunk and sat down on the floor. He knew, just as surely as he was sitting there, that it was going to be empty, but when he opened it, he saw that he'd been left something. Picking up the penny, shiny and coppery, he thought of all the things he was going to do with it.

"First, I'm going to shove it up his ass. Then I might go find it, heat it up, and burn it into his skull." Getting up now, pacing the floor, he thought of many more things that he wanted to do. How he was going to use this small token as a parting gift for the man and his family. "I'm going to get that man, make him pay. Today. I've lost everything because of him. Everything."

In the back of his mind, he knew that wasn't true. He'd had nothing to do with the building, nor the money that had been down there. It had, until this morning, been Lewis's to do with as he wanted. But he'd known, last night when he'd agreed to sell it to him, that the money had been here, and that Byron was hoping to get it. That in and of itself was enough to make his temper short. It was a dirty trick...no matter how it had happened. He'd been taken to the cleaners by a McCade, and he was going to make them pay for their shit.

Chapter 8

Butler had found himself a new home. Not that it was much better than the one that he'd had before, but at least this one had a roof that completely covered it, as well as a fireplace that he could light up when he got cold. And he found that as his magic wore off, he would get chilled at the slightest breeze. As he moved around the place, careful not to use any of his magic to make improvements, he thought of the pain he'd gotten yesterday when his shifter had been returned to him.

"Didn't even know that could be done."

The laughter made him pause, and he looked around. "Who's there? What are you about?"

Children had taken to tormenting him. Not that he could do anything about it, but he thought that once he'd hit one of them in the head with a rock, the others would scatter. But all it did was make them come back in droves. It was another reason that he'd moved here...to get away from the little shits.

To think that he'd spent some of his magic on the shifter to kill him a McCade, and all it had done was piss it away. The laughter again had him hiding now. He wasn't sure what was there, or who might be trying to find him, but he needed to take steps in keeping himself safe. Butler hoped to all heavens that it wasn't his wife again. She had never learned her place.

"Hello, Father." His son stood before him, and all he could think about was the last meeting that they'd had. It had been decades ago, just after he'd managed to kill the third woman that had come to the dragons. "I see you are not faring well. I'm not unhappy about that. If you were to just die, as you should have done many years ago, I could easily live a much happier life."

"What a thing to say to your own father. Come here, give me a hug." Caelin only stood there, with the light shining on him from the open doorway. "Nothing to give me, Caelin my boy? What is a sire to think when his own kin won't spare a hug for him?"

"So that you might stab me in the back? Or were you going to aim for my heart?" The knife that he had hidden in his pocket was suddenly quivering on the floor between his feet. "Come now, you must know that I'm smarter than you'll ever be. And since I know that you're not long for this world, I know for a fact that you'll get no smarter either."

"Did your mother not raise you to have respect for your elders?" He said that she'd done a fine job raising him, and that was one of the first lessons that she'd taught him. "Well, I've seen none of it. I think you have forgotten more than you learned. But then, she is nothing more than a female, not worth much unless you can sell her off."

"I have four daughters." Butler laughed, thinking him having the same curse as he'd been given. "But I also have six boys. Sons that are strong and good. Taking care of their parents in their age so that we no longer have to work as hard. And grandchildren too, to bounce upon our knees whenever we wish to see them. You might well have had that, Father, should you have been a little kinder."

"Children are for fools, or to have them bring you a coin. What did you do with your daughters? Keep them in your home until a time they fell in love for themselves? Blah. Love, too, is nothing but an emotion that only women, and fools, have. Are you a fool, Caelin?" He said nothing. "I would have taken you on hunts. Showed you how to be a man of men. They would have trembled to have heard you coming. And bowed before you when you walked by them. Men would have looked upon me as a great father, but for your mother."

"You think so? I don't. And if you call me a fool because I loved my wife and children, then you go right ahead, Father." He said that like a curse. Like the word father meant no more to him than the dirt beneath his boots. "You may have your opinions, Father, they mean very little to me and mine, but I am here to strike a deal with you. You leave the McCades alone, and I will not allow you to die slowly, but make your death, when it comes, quick and nearly painless."

"You think to kill me? Your own father, Caelin?" He laughed. Butler was actually afraid that if it came to that, his son could easily do so. "I'm not afeared of you, my boy. I know that you cannot kill me without good reason. And I have given

113

you none."

"You think not? I find the opposite to be true. You have given me many reasons to kill you. Even by today's standards of living, you are a man on death row." He hadn't any idea what that meant, but said nothing. But Caelin knew he didn't understand, and explained it him anyway. "It means a man that is going to lose his head for his crimes and deeds. You have a long list of them, Father. Longer than I thought a man could have but the fact that you're losing everything, that makes me happy. Anyway, a bargain. You wish to hear the terms?"

"You can say them, but I shan't leave them to their own. I aim to rule, Caelin, with or without you at my side. Name your terms. I'd like to hear what foolery you have come up with that you think I should do." He sat down on the chair closest to him. Butler couldn't remember one being there, and had a thought that Caelin would take it from him. But when it did nothing but groan under his weight, he told him to continue.

"All right. I will pay you, a great sum of money. Not that you deserve any, but I shall nonetheless." He shook his head. Whatever money he might pay him was going to be very little compared to what he would have when he had the dragon. "I will also make sure that you're an immortal, for all time."

"I'm immortal now. You must do better than that, Caelin. You have said nothing that would entice me to come over to your way of thinking." He waved his hand at his son, telling him to go on. "Anything more?"

"Plenty, but I would also like to point out that you're no longer immortal, are you, Father? But a man who is on his last bit of magic, and even that is betraying him." Caelin sat too, in

114

a magnificent chair of velvet and gold. "Are you still in pain? Does your belly even now leak out what some would consider blood? Does it wake you in the night? How about when your shifter was returned to you? Honestly, I had no idea that it could be done either, but she did it, didn't she?"

"Who? Who did this?" Caelin only laughed. "I demand that you tell me who killed a creature of my making. You will tell me, Caelin, or I shall run you through."

Butler leaned forward, to settle in the chair a little easier for his belly's sake, when the blade suddenly in his son's hand touched his nose. How he'd gotten across the room and drawn his sword so quickly was something that scared him and thrilled him too. To have such power would be wonderful.

"You will not make demands of me, Father. Nor will you threaten me again." He nodded, afeared once again of his son. "When will you learn that I am far stronger than you are? That I hold all the magic that came with the castle, simply because my mother made sure of it. And someday soon it will rise again, and you will never see it."

"You think me to be killed by your kin? I don't know if you're aware of this or not, young Caelin, but as king, I can call the dragon long before they get their heads out of their asses and figure out how to do it." Caelin said nothing. Here was a face that he'd never play a game of chance with; he gave no visible signs of what he was thinking. "Why don't you concede to me? Have them give me the pieces that they now have, and I'll let them live. For a bit longer, at least."

"They cannot die." He asked him what he meant. "They're immortals. True immortals, in that nothing will kill them. None of them, nor those that they bring to their hearts. I thought you should know that, in the event that you think to kill one of them now."

"No, you don't have the power to do that." Caelin shrugged. "Well, it matters little. I will come out on top of this all. You wait and see. I have plans that no one knows about."

"If you believe so. So you are going to turn down my offers? You have no wish for the money or magic?" Butler started to tell him no, but thought of something that he'd like to have. "I'm not going to heal you, Father. That is going to be your downfall, you being hurt. I wish all the time that I'd been able to kill you then, but I know that things must be done in order. And you dying by my hand, it will be of little use to them. No, I'm not going to give you any magic to use."

"You are an ungrateful cur, that's what you are. Nothing more than a little piss of a thing that your mother was too ashamed to bring to me when you were birthed." He wanted to see him angry, to see if his temper matched his own, but all he did was laugh, like he had no cares in the world at all. "Are you such a pussy whipped being that you will not allow yourself to grow angry, boy? You're much like your mother, I think. Do you whelp children too? Nurse them, perhaps?"

"If you're trying to anger me, it won't work. Not about my children nor wife. I love them, and would do anything for them. And with them. I will not engage with you on that level." He asked him what it would take for him to be angered. "Nothing you can say or do will make me mad. I am a man with a purpose, a plan that will end this between us once and for all."

"You think that, do you? And what am I to do, Caelin?

Allow it to happen? To let you, like your mother did, take everything from me? I won't. I will see you both dead before I will be duped again. By anyone." He nearly reached up to touch his part in all this, the necklace that would give him it all. "Be gone with you. I have no desire to waste my breath talking to a momma's boy who is no more a son to me than one of my daughters was."

"Yes, I can see that, Father." He wanted to get up and slap the boy — a man really — but didn't want to be hurt. His son, so much like his mother that he would have hated him no matter how this turned out. Even his looks, fine bones, and hair, made Butler envious of him. There wasn't an ounce of fat on him, and he looked as fit as anyone that he'd ever encountered. With his body dressed in the modern-day clothing, he could have passed for one of those men that were on the cover of paper books he'd seen. The ones where they were holding a beautiful half-dressed woman.

After his son left him, Butler needed to lie down. However, he'd not been out looking for things, so had neither a bed nor a chair to sit his body in. Even the chair that had been his for the seating was gone, in its place a pile of rubble like that of his former house.

He needed to get to one of the women. Just one. And once he had her in his hands, the others would fall apart. Butler knew women and the way that they led men around by their dicks. Especially this generation of them. Once he was able to get the woman, any of them, in his clutches, he'd have the entire set, and then there would be hell to pay. As much as he hated waiting around, the need to find a witch to give him what he needed was well past time. That had to be his first duty, to end this. Butler was going to win, and then they'd see what he was about.

~~~

The wedding was beautiful, and the guests seemed to be enjoying the food. Lewis had outdone himself on this, and the cake that Emma had made was a masterpiece. Everything, right down to the decorations on the tables, was just what she'd wanted. Aisha walked to her son and hugged him to her.

"You did it." He said that he couldn't get over the cake. "Yes, me either. Did you have any idea that she was going to make it into a castle with a dragon climbing up the side? My goodness, Lewis. I know that most of the people here haven't any idea of the connection, but we do, and I cannot believe that she did this. It's far better than I could have hoped for. And the food. You should be serving these sort of items all the time."

"Mostly I will be, and a few others. When we open tomorrow night, we're only going to start with a few meals. I have beef stroganoff, and chicken alfredo for those who don't care for red meat." Aisha told him that was an excellent plan. "Since we're all getting our feet wet with this wedding, I'm going to also start slow in the restaurant. There will be wine, of course. As well as bread and salads. Desserts too, thanks to Emma, but the rest will be testing mode. I don't want to overwhelm anyone."

"We'll be here." Lewis kissed her on the cheek. "I have one more thing I have in store for you. I've gone ahead and planned your wedding out as well. I thought that there wasn't a better time than today to get you two hitched up."

"We were married this morning." She glared at him. "It was

118

my idea, so you can't blame anyone but me. After this thing with Clayton, I thought that Raven should be really married to me instead of just my saying so, in case he gets nasty."

"That man is going to go to prison if he doesn't watch himself. I heard that he'd made a big stink at the bank this afternoon too. About how you'd been in his place before the papers were signed. He didn't own it until then, so what's the big deal?" Lewis told her that he'd not been in the place since before he'd had dinner with the man. "Well, I'm glad you did it the way you did. Things would have gone better had there not been a murder too, but I think you and Raven have done good by the man. I don't really care what he thinks happened, he needs to rein himself in."

She knew about the money. They all did, as a matter of fact. It was going to go for a lot of good causes, and she was happy that they'd had a nice service for the dead man too. He wasn't a nice person, not from what she'd overheard the boys talking about, but he was buried now, in a good place, and that was the end of it. The fact that he'd left behind all the money was just karma to her. And they were going to make very good use of it.

"I was thinking that we'd set aside a fund for you to use as well. For book bags and such. Grady said he'd run it for you, keeping the books and all. And that when it came time to add to it, the fundraisers that you hold would just make it so that many more kids can get a good start." She hugged him. "Did you know that Jasmine and Gabe are working it so that there is hot food for the kids in the morning instead of just a box of cereal? Also, a coat drive has been put on the books for the kids. We might not have been able to do that had it not been for this

119

man."

"Yes, he's done a lot of people up right." They watched as Dalton and Gabe moved around the room talking to people. "I'm so proud of you all. I just wish Vance could have been here to see the reception. I can't wait for him to stop this nonsense and be at home more."

"I think that is his plan too." Aisha knew that they thought she had no idea what Vance was up to. Well, she didn't know all of it, but she knew enough that she worried for him. He worked for the government, and was in trouble with someone higher up. Who, she didn't know, but she knew that Vance was planning to take care of that as well. "Mom, Gavin and you, you guys have been doing some amazing things lately. I was wondering if the two of you would do me a favor. I need someone to help with the animals that we have on the farm."

"You have a farm?" He nodded and told her about the goats and donkeys they had. As well as the unicorn. "I think I'd like to come out and see them soon. A unicorn. Had you asked me, I would have said they didn't exist. Yes, we can help you. What is it you think you need from us?"

"The donkeys are going to have foals soon, before winter. I want to make it so that they can have kids come out and see them." She looked at him with a million questions in her mind. "I think it would do some of the handicapped a world of good to come out and pet a few animals, don't you? And Raven is going to see about getting a couple of smaller animals. Chickens, and perhaps a cow or two. We'll be a real farm in no time."

"My son, the farmer." They both laughed. "I'm wondering if anytime soon you'll be serving up goat cheese and the like."

"That's the plan." Again she was astonished by him. When he hugged her and left, she went in search of Raven. That girl had made her quiet son into someone that she liked. Not that she didn't love him before, but now he nearly glowed with happiness. As soon as she hugged her, Aisha knew something was wrong.

"What is it? What do I need to do to help you hide the body? Or bodies." They both laughed, and she could have sworn that there was a touch of sadness in Raven's eyes. "Raven, honey, what is it? You can tell me anything."

"I know that. And you're the best mother-in-law a woman could have." She hugged her again, and Aisha felt better. "I want to warn you about something. It's important, so I want you to listen."

"I don't want to know." Raven told her that she'd be safer if she did. "I can't be killed, and I have my family right here with me. Not Vance though, but the rest of you. And I have another daughter-in-law coming. I couldn't be happier. Anything you tell me, or warn me about, it's just going to depress me, and I don't want that."

"He's going to take you." She asked her who. "Byron Clayton. He's going to take you tonight, and you need to be prepared for it. As soon as you leave here."

"This isn't the first time someone has tried this." She said that she knew that. "All right. Do I need to have a posse with me? Do I need to get my gun out now?"

"No. I'd like for you to let him take you. He won't mean to hurt you if you resist, but if you go with him, wherever it is, we'll find you. But when he takes you, he'll be breaking the law. And everything will be back to where it should be." Aisha wasn't sure what that meant, but told her she'd go with him. "Good. And when you're free of him, I'd like to give you a little magic to keep you safer, if you don't mind."

"All right. I'm not even going to ask what it is. You just give it to me and I'll try not to kill anyone.... Is that why you're waiting for me to get it after he takes me? You're afraid that I'll kill him?" Raven nodded. "That bird of yours, he's been keeping an eye on me too, hasn't he? I have to tell you, child, he scares me a little. Not that he's ever tried to harm me, but he talks, and that takes some getting used to."

"Yes. But I have to tell you, he thinks that you hate him." She said that she didn't. "I know that, and you do, but he doesn't. Poe, for all his magic, is a very insecure little guy. I love him to pieces, but he wants, more than anything, for you to like him, even a little."

"How would I go about that? Making him sure that I like him?" She put out her hand when asked to and looked down at the kernels of corn. "That's all? Just give him some corn? I can do that."

"Not just corn, though that is one of his favorites. But even just talking to him when he's near you. Call him to where you are. He's very tame, and won't ever harm you." Raven laughed. "He thinks himself a good chess player. Do you play?" She said that she did, but wasn't all that good at it. "Neither is he, but he loves to think that he is."

She was thinking about that as she left the restaurant. What would people think if they saw her sitting on her front porch, playing chess with a big raven? Laughing at the sight they'd make, she didn't hear the person come up behind her until he grabbed her from behind. When she turned to look at him, it scared her to no end to see the insanity in Byron's eyes.

"You're coming with me." She nodded at him and told him not to hurt her. "Like I care if you get a few cuts and bruises. That son of yours, he took something that belonged to me, and I want you to get it back for me."

"Get what back for you?" He told her to mind her own business. That had her pissed off. "You are making me come with you under some guise of getting back at my son for some reason, and you don't think that's any of my business? You need to have your head examined if you think that's going to fly with any of my boys. What is this all about?"

"There was money in that building he sold me, and I want it back." Aisha crossed her arms over her chest and waited for him to continue. "I had plans for that money, and he took it."

"So? What do you think he's going to do when he finds out that you kidnapped his mom? Do you think he's going to walk up to you and say, 'Sorry, Byron, here's your money. Please let my mom go.' No, he's going to hurt you. More than likely kill you. And then what are you going to do with that money? Nothing...you'll be dead, you moron."

"It's mine." She hit him much like she would have one of her own sons when they were being stupid. "I have a gun. I will use it on you."

"No you don't. Had you a gun you would have waved it around like you would your dick, trying to impress a woman. Let me tell you, young man, I do not impress easily. Now, what do you think about this plan? You let me go, and I won't say a word to anyone about how stupid you are." He told her to shut up. "You have a lot of orders for someone that is trying to keep you alive."

"I want that money." She told him that his idea was going to get him killed. "No, no it won't. I'll leave the country. Buy me a boat and maybe an island, where I can live happily ever after."

Aisha slapped him across the face hard. And when he hit the ground, she put her booted foot on his chest and held him there. The nerve of some people. When he started to rise up, she told him to stay still or she'd ram her heel into his heart and kill him herself.

"You're a fool, Byron Clayton. Your momma, God rest her poor old soul, would be embarrassed to see what you're up to. That money is going to a lot of good causes. Coats for kids. A hot meal or two for some people that won't otherwise have any. Perhaps a suit for a job interview, as well as helping someone out on their bills. You should be happy that he found it before you. It would never have made you as happy as it will the people that will use it." Byron told her that Lewis would use it for himself. "No, that's what you were going to do with it. You know my sons well enough to know that they'd never steal anything to help themselves. And you know as well as I do that money belonged to Lewis. You should have reported it instead of letting the poor man lie there without a care in the world."

"I lost everything." She looked up and saw that Raven and Lewis were in front of the rest of her family. "I have nothing left. I used it all to get that building."

"I tell you what, Byron. You come and work for my family,

124

for that money. You see what it can do for people who have done without for so long. You help them spend it helping others, and I'll help you get back on your feet." He looked at her, and she could see that he'd been crying. "I'll help you, Byron, if you help yourself."

"Why would you do that? I was going to kidnap you and hurt you for that money." She said that there was enough violence going on in the world. "I don't know what to do, Mrs. McCade. I really did bet everything on that cash."

"Well, now you can bet everything on helping spend it. In the right way." He nodded, and she put out her hand to help him up. "Byron, I don't offer my hand to many people, so you'd better take it and what I'm offering you. I'd surely hate to have to explain to the cops on my son's wedding day how I had to kill a man before he hurt me."

When he was upright, she hugged him to her. Of all the hugs she'd gotten tonight, she thought this one meant the most to her. A man down on his luck, like so many others were, had been as close to hurting her as her own husband used to, and she'd been able to walk away without having to put a bullet in his head. Thinking of that, she put her gun back in her pocket book and joined Byron in the restaurant for some food. Aisha was glad now that she'd been warned. She might have shot first and talked later had she not.

Chapter 9

"You hired a man that was going to kidnap you for the money that rightfully belonged to me. I don't understand why you would do something like that." Lewis looked at Raven. She'd been smiling since Byron had shown up at the restaurant last evening. "You can't think this is a good idea. Do you?"

"Yes. What were you going to use the money for? To give people a hand up, correct?" He didn't like her logic. "What better way to prove to someone that you're going to do just that than to hire a man who was more down on his luck than most, and desperate enough to maybe kill someone."

"This is insane. The both of you are." Lewis looked at his mom when she cleared her throat. "You are not going to reprimand me when you have done something like this. What if he had shot you, then what would you have done? Given him the keys to your car to drive off with?"

He knew he'd gone too far when Mom stood up...she was

not one to fuck around with. But instead of backing down, or even letting her hit him in the forehead like she was known to do, he hugged her to him. Tightly, making sure that her hands were between them.

"Oh, Lewis. Don't think for a moment that you've gotten the better of me with this move. I knew just what I was doing." He looked down at her and she smiled. "He needed this much more than we could have imagined, son. I saw the look in his eyes. They were not just desperate, as you said, but insane too."

"You're not helping this at all, you know." She pulled from him and went to the cabinets. When she reached into the first one, he knew just what she was looking for. "The brew is over here in the crock jars. There are different kinds, I've learned, depending on what your mood is. What is your mood right now?"

"Murdering you." Lewis pointed out that was an action, not a mood, and she hit him anyway. "I am stressed out, if you need to know. I didn't have any idea why I hired him. But it seemed the right thing to do. Tell me something, Lewis…what would you have done, had he tried to take you, or Raven? What would you have done?"

"First of all, Raven can take care of herself." He winked at his new wife. "Secondly, while I'm aware of how strong you are, and how willful you are, you are still, and will forever be, my mom. A woman who I know killed a man when he tried his best to kill me."

Lewis kissed her forehead and asked her to have a seat while he brewed them all a cup of tea. There was a great deal going on now; the restaurant was opening tonight, Butler was going to try and hurt one of them, and his brother Vance was going to be leaving soon…and they'd not know until it was over if he succeeded or not. Yes, a great deal was on all their plates, he thought, but his mom was first in this.

"I need for him…. No…he needs to work with me in getting this money going to the right places. Yes, he did try and swindle you, and he did try and kidnap me, but those are things he tried to do. Not succeeded at. He's a good man, Lewis. You don't like him, I know, but he's a good man. Raven told me so." Lewis looked at Raven and she nodded. "See. He's going to be just fine."

"He won't." Lewis closed his eyes when Raven spoke quietly, knowing that it was going to be bad news. "He's a good man that is going to die before he is too much older. Not that there is much that can be done for him at this point, but to work for you, it will give him something that he's never had before…pride in himself. He will die; not soon, but in the next ten years, at peace with his actions that he's taken on with you and this family."

"He'll work for us." His mom patted him on the hand when he spoke. "I don't have to like it, but I would hate to have him feel like he's failed at anything when he didn't hurt you."

"Good for you. I'm very proud of you. Both of you." When she sat down again, he knew that she was going to ask about Vance. He had no idea why, so when she did, he had an answer for her.

"He said that he was going to take care of some business. That's all I can tell you." She frowned at him. "I'll tell you the same thing you told me a while back. He's immortal. He cannot die, so you don't have to worry overly much about him."

"That's good to think about, but he is my baby, all of you are, and I don't want any of you hurt. Not even to scratch yourself." Mom sat there for several more minutes before she got up. "I have to go and meet with Gavin this morning. We're already planning next year's event, and working on the one for October. That one will be the biggest fund raiser that we've ever had."

"Aisha, why not really up the ticket sales?" Mom asked Raven how to do that. "Take some of this money and buy a new truck. I'd try to get a good deal on it first, but why not do that? I'm sure there are a great many people that would buy a ticket or two more for the chance to win a new car."

"Oh, I love that idea. You'd not believe the donations that we have, but that could be the topper." Mom looked at him again. "What do you think? Would that be all right with you?"

"Mom, whatever she wants, I'm fine with it. It's the family money as far as I'm concerned, and if you two agree, then I'm all for it." He laughed when Mom winked at him. "I will buy the first tickets for it. Put me down for a hundred of them. And if I win, I'll donate it to the shelter, so they can use it to get groceries and supplies."

He knew by the end of the day not only would his brothers all buy tickets too, but they'd buy more just to outdo him. Laughing as he made his way to his car, he stopped when he saw Ralph Donavan standing near the garage, and went to talk to the younger man.

"Everything all right?" He nodded and grinned at him. "Then why are you stalking my garage, and not coming in and talking to my wife and mom?"

"Your mom scares me and most of my pack. She does a lot for us, but she can be a little intense when things aren't going her way. Or what she thinks she wants." He asked if things were going to upset her. "Not that I know of, but you never can tell. I'm here for a different reason. The goats and such that you have here, we were wondering if we could add a few animals to the pens as well. There are a few members of the pack, younger children, who would like to be able to put them in the county fair for next fall. You can say no, should you not want to bother, but they said that they'd clean out stalls and come by and feed them for you for the usage."

Raven joined him then, and he told her what Donavan wanted to do. "Wonderful. I love that idea. But I am going to add some chickens, as well as a few other animals. If they tell me what they want to show, I can purchase it for them for my stock as well."

"Thank you. These kids, they've taken a keen interest in school of late. Most of them, the younger kids, they're bored and get into trouble easily. I was hoping with this project for them, they'd be less inclined to get into trouble." Raven and Donavan were still talking when he went to his car again.

Lewis had a lot to do at the restaurant for their grand opening today. When he'd left last night, he'd only had about four tables reserved, which was fine by him. It would give his staff time to ease into their different jobs. Even his second chefs, two of them from the college and one a member of the pack that was going to be helping with ordering, were happy with the way things had gone yesterday.

As soon as he walked in, he got to work. There was soup to make, and decisions to make about what sort of appetizers they were going to serve. Tonight only, he had decided to let people have a small plate of them, as a tester to see what would go over well. Then the hostess, another member of the pack, was going to ask what they enjoyed most on the plate. That way, he figured, he'd get a good accounting of things.

"Hey, Lewis, we need to talk." Lewis looked at Patty, his hostess for tonight. He was sure she was going to quit on him. "The phone has been ringing since I got here, and I wanted to talk to you about an answering machine or a service. That way we can put it on, so I can help out."

"Okay, I can see that. But how many people could be calling now? I mean, we don't open for...." He looked at the clock. "We don't even open for at least eight more hours. Why are they calling so early?"

"Reservations. I have tonight filled up, and a waiting list. Also, we've decided—the staff and I—that we're going to set a few of the extra tables that are in the back outside for those that want to eat out of doors tonight." He told her they could hold over a hundred and fifty people. "Yes, well, we'll be able to accommodate at least a dozen more outside. Twice over, that's a good number of people. And I've called some extra help in here to wait tables."

"We can hold over a hundred and fifty people, Patty." She laughed and said she was aware of that. "I don't understand. Last night we had four reservations. Are you saying now that all the tables are full?"

"Twice." He shook his head while she nodded. "I know

132

what I'm doing, Lewis. Trust me on this. You are going to be fine."

"I wasn't planning on this. I might...I need to go to the store." She told him he'd better hurry then. "Are you sure about this? I mean, this isn't a joke, is it?"

"I don't joke about my job. You know that. You're going to be fine. You'll be a hit, and we'll be this busy every night. I know it." She started away, then turned back. "You might want to rethink giving away the plate of food tonight. It might be too much for you. But if you want, I can have the staff tell them about one or two of them verbally. That way the opening menu won't have to be reprinted."

Stepping away from the prep table, he stood there with his mind simply blank. When someone said his name, he looked at Raven and shook his head. He didn't know what she said, but he wasn't able to speak to her just then. Then she hit him.

"What was that for?" She told him he was freaking out. "Yes, but to hit me means I have to do something to you. Like.... I have over three hundred people coming to dinner tonight. And a town this size? That's about ten percent of them. Coming here. To eat at my place."

"Good for you." She was nodding, but he was shaking his head. "Yes, good for you. I can help too. What kind of things do you want me to do?"

"I need more food. I mean, a lot of it. Chickens, as well as steaks. I need to get more salad fixings as well.... What are you doing now? Having a list made for me?" She said she'd go with someone, and he'd be able to get things done here. "I don't know what else I need."

"Am I going to have to call your mom here?" He smiled and told her no. "Good. Okay, what sort of salad fixings? I'm assuming you don't mean just lettuce and such."

When she left him an hour later, he'd gone through the walk-in, the pantry, as well as the freezer. There was a great deal for her to get for him, so he had her take his dishwashers to help, as well as someone to direct her around the store and to drive. Lewis decided that he would work on one thing at a time, get it done, and not think about anything else. As soon as he had a plan, he thought he might be just fine.

"Who am I kidding? I'm going to royally fuck this up."

~~~

Caelin stayed hidden as he watched the restaurant. There were so many people coming and going that he knew tonight was going to be a success for his grandson. Listening to the people as they came out, he was happy to hear that they really were surprised at how good everything was, and that they'd be returning. Caelin loved these little moments in time, when he could marvel that someone he had helped create, a grandchild of many generations past, was making a go at something. He turned to look at Raven when she stood beside him.

"You're in love." She nodded, and told him that she was very much in love. "I'm so glad. You deserve it more than most, I think."

He thought about the magic that she'd helped him with. All the times that she'd been there for him. It never came between them that his own father had done this to her, or that Butler had killed her mother as well. Raven was just kind hearted, a good friend as well as someone that he'd come to love like he did one

134

of his own children.

"I have a gift for you." She said that she didn't want a gift from him. He was kind enough to her. "You always say that. Even when I give you something for your birthday. It is coming up, you know."

"I do. As is yours. We have the same date, though you are a bit older than me." She laughed. "Not that I'm keeping track, however."

"You know just how old we both are, and it matters little. I'm so very glad to see you as happy as you are now." Nodding, they stood there for a few moments without speaking. "My wife, she said to tell you that she'd like some more of your brew. We have another great.... I have no idea how many greats it is now, but we have another coming."

"It would be my pleasure to help you both. I like your wife." It took him a moment to realize that she'd made a joke, something that she wasn't prone to do. "Butler is coming, Caelin. And when he comes here, he will die."

"Yes, that is the plan. And Vance will do it. He has been the hardest to get a good eye on. I worry for him." She asked if his mate would help him. "In ways that you cannot imagine. She is going to be his sanity, as well as his balance. I think she might even knock him to his ass a few times before this is done."

"He will never harm her." Caelin said he knew that as well. "What will you do with yourself when you no longer have to plot and plan the lives of all of these people? I think you will be very bored in your golden years. What say you? Will you take that lovely wife of yours on a long vacation? A cruise, perhaps?"

"I do have a plan. I'm going to sit under your large oak

135

tree and have myself a nap. It has been far too long since I've been able to do something like that." He looked at the people enjoying life to the fullest. "You should be having this sort of enjoyment too, my friend."

"I am enjoying my life. I have my goats and donkeys. Also, we now have chickens, as well as two pigs. I wasn't sure that Lewis would want them around — they do smell — but he wants me to have what I need. I never thought that I'd find someone so loving and wonderful to me." He said once again that she deserved it. "I think you might be right."

"What? You are agreeing with me? My goodness. What ever shall I do now?" He touched his fingers to her cheek, just a small touch that would mean nothing to anyone else, but he gave her magic, a little something that he wished he'd been able to do so long ago. "I must go now. When I return, it will not be a social call. It will mean that the end is coming. I would very much like to come and stay with you and Lewis as well, and bring my wife."

"We'd love that. I know that the family would like to get to know you. And then the castle will need to be visited. I have in mind that you've been there aplenty." He said that he had, especially of late. "Is it coming along then?"

"Better than we had hoped, I think. And once this is finished, all will be well." Caelin started to tell her that he knew she had the necklace, but decided that he'd leave that for another time. It was as safe as it could be with her. Kissing her on the cheek, he gave her just a little more and knew that Lewis would benefit from it as well.

Caelin made his way to his castle and marveled at what

had been repaired for the family. Not only were most of the walls up and stronger than before, but even the hiding place, the one that he'd been keeping from everyone, was cleaned up and nearly complete. Going there now, he thought of his dear mother.

"You were good to me. And made me what I am today." Getting down on his knees, he pulled the silken cloth off her portrait and looked at her face. "You were so beautiful, Mother. I miss you more and more every day. And the closer we get to the end of this, I look forward to seeing you again."

"You know that I cannot come to you." He said that he understood, but to see her would be good for him for now. "You always were such a demanding brat, weren't you?"

Caelin laughed and turned to look at the image of his mother. She wasn't there — she could never be there until the child was born — but he could see and talk to her like this. Sitting down, he told her of all the things that were being done.

"The restaurant, it's doing well then?" He told her of the comments that he'd heard when the guests were leaving. "I have high hopes for them. Not just because I've a softness for Lewis — he does look like you a great deal — but for young Raven as well. She has a special place in my heart."

"I have given her sight back to her. She will find out when she wakes two mornings from now. It is well past time. Her voyage to Lewis was what kept me from doing it before now. But she will need it, when the children come to them." His mother sat too, but not on anything where he was. "Also, the children that are coming to the others, I have taken care that things go well for the mothers. They would heal quickly

137

anyway, but there is no need for them to suffer overly much when I can help. It was my own wife that suggested it."

"I would like to meet her someday as well. And my grandchildren." He nodded. They had missed so much, being parted the way that they had been. "Oh, Caelin. I am so very proud of you. And all that you've done. I could not have asked for a better son."

"You taught me well, Mother. Had you not, I would never have survived those first years." He had been in hiding for five years when his mother disappeared. "And Warrior, he is helping as much as he can. Mostly he keeps Lewis and Vance calm. Especially Vance."

"I would imagine that he will be glad for his mate when she comes to him." Caelin said he wasn't sure about that. "Why not? A woman to balance him? Someone that would be his equal? Vance, of all the men in that family, he is the most wounded. And I don't mean his body. Though I have seen it. He has been hurt a great deal."

"His heart will be hard to get into, I'm afraid. And easily broken. When she gets there, I think she will be just as hard. They are a pair, the two of them." His mother said she knew that too. "I have not given them any information on her. And Warrior cannot. Since she won't touch the piece until she is with them, I think her to be the safest I can make her. That doesn't mean that she won't have troubles, mostly of her own making. But at least Father won't be able to track her. If he tries. He believes he still has the piece you left behind."

"Does Raven know you are aware that she took it?" He shook his head. "Good. I think that, for the time being, it would be better if she kept it from you. Should your father find a witch to help him, you know that he would be able to see it in your mind."

"Yes. I'm aware. Does he see another witch? I have looked, but it is blocked from me." His mother didn't answer, not that he thought she would. "I have a bit of news for you that you might like. My son, he is going to live in the area with the McCades. His plan is to take over one of the shops in town and sell his carvings. This keeps up and the town will be known wide and far for the artists that live there."

"I have missed so much." He was sorry then that he'd brought it up. "No, don't do that. I wish to hear all about them all. You will keep me updated on all that goes on, and while it does sadden me at times, I do love knowing that life, no matter how fragile it is, still moves on with you and yours."

He pulled out his phone, a new device for himself, and showed her every picture he'd taken. Some of them were a little out of focus—he was still getting used to using it—but she enjoyed them, just as much as he did. And when she was tiring, just as he was, he told her again how much he loved her and was looking forward to seeing her again.

"You must bring your wife the next time you come. I should so like to see her." He told her that he would, but after his newest great grandchild was born. "Bring it as well. Just to let me gaze upon it and see if it looks like you do."

"It's a boy. He is going to be a strong boy, and a full dragon too. That will make seven hundred of them now, just in my family alone." He smiled when she clapped her hands. "Soon, Mother dear. Soon, we'll all be together."

He left the cavern then, making his way into the darkening night. There wasn't much for him to do now. All that could be done to keep them safe was finished. Just the one woman, a woman of great hope for them all, was to come yet. But there were other things, things to do with Vance, which would need to be started first. Laughing to himself, he thought of the two of them together. And knew for as long as he lived, that Vance would begin to hate him or love him because of her. She was going to be a trial to them all.

The house was coming into view when he saw the man in the pasture. It wasn't anything for them to have people going into the fields and taking a few pieces of fruit or something that was growing there. He watched him for several minutes as he filled a bag of oranges and apples. They didn't normally grow around this area, but his lady wife liked them, so he'd put them in the ground. Just as he was to approach the man, to see if he needed anything else, he saw the two children.

Caelin had a soft spot for children, and he hated to see them abused or hungry. Coming out of his hiding place, he reached out to the man, to see the sort of man he was, and found that he, like his children, was starving. The fruit would go a long way in filling his children's bellies, but the man would not eat until they were full. It was a quality that gave him an instant liking of the man.

"I meant no harm to you and yours, my lord." Caelin nodded as the man dropped the fruit and had his children scatter. "I only wanted them to have a treat."

"Come to my home, sir, and enjoy a meal with us. Then when you have fed well, we'll see about finding you a job and

140

a place to live." The man started crying, his body dropping to the ground with the fruit. The children came back to hold their upset father, and Caelin knelt to them. "Come on now. We'll see about getting you a hot meal, some blankets and things. My wife, she is a good cook."

"You don't know us. I could be a monster in sheep's clothing. Why would you do such a thing?" Caelin led him to the house, warning his wife that they were to have company. "I would only see that the children are fed, sir. Thank you for that."

"You'll all eat and stay the night. I insist." He picked up the fruit. "Maybe my wife can make us a fine dessert with this. And the rest, you can take to your home."

He fixed them a place to live. Found Wendel a job and someone to help him in his home. The children were too thin, but with his help and that of his family, that would soon be taken care of as well. Caelin was sitting to his own supper when his wife kissed him on the back of the head, telling him that she loved him.

"And I love you as well, my heart." He finished his meal and sat with her while she knitted. They were content, for now, and he could not be happier.

Chapter 10

Lewis stood very still. He could feel something in the area, but had no idea what it might be. And when Poe landed on his shoulder, he knew that the raven had felt it as well. Asking him what it was in a whisper, the raven squawked once and nodded in the general direction of the cave before them.

"'Tis a dragon, my lord. One that you were told about." He asked if he was all right. "Nay, I think him to be exhausted, but he needs only to rest for a bit, then he'll make himself known to you and Raven."

"Can I take him anything? Water? Food? I don't know what he might eat, but I'd gladly take it to him." Poe told him that the cave had a spring in it, and it was full of fish. The earth had given the dragon all that she had. "Okay, that's good. Is he a big dragon?"

"Yes. About as big as your truck." That wasn't as large as he'd thought, but it would be hard to hide him should someone

143

come around. "He's magical, my lord, as all dragons are. His name is Darmor, and he is quite old."

"But you are sure that he's all right? The reason I ask is, I feel something off. Not right." Poe didn't understand. "When the shifter came to me, I could smell it. Evilness. I smell it again. Close to where we are."

"Then perhaps we should check on him. I don't want him to be harmed after coming this far to be with you." Lewis didn't either, but he didn't know how much help he'd be to a large-as-his-truck dragon that was tired. "Shall we go?"

The cave was warmer than he'd thought it would be. Also, it was dry. He wondered aloud about that, and was told by Poe that it was the dragon, warming it up where he was, and it dried the air. Which, he supposed, made sense. But the deeper they went into the cave, the heat of it was almost too much. About a mile into the cave, Lewis smelled it again.

"Here. Whatever is around, it's here. Where is the dragon now?" Poe moved off his shoulder and down the dark cave. When he returned, he looked concerned. "What is it?"

"Someone has put a spell on him." Again, Lewis hadn't any idea what that might mean, but he hurried after the bird when he went back down the cave. "I have called to Raven. She is coming by her magic. Also, Lord Kenton is coming. I know not if he can help, but perhaps he can tell us what we can do for the dragon."

The dragon was indeed large, and he was sick. As Darmor was sick again, he stood back. The poor animal was just lying down again when Kenton and Raven showed up. Kenton didn't look happy either.

"Remind me never to come by way of magic with your wife again." He asked him what had happened, and Raven called him a baby. "She is blind, and the fact that she told me she hoped that we'd not end up in a rock was not funny."

Lewis was still laughing when the dragon looked at him. Putting his hand on his head, he told him that he was there for him. That was when his touch brought who had done this to his mind.

"Butler did this." The dragon nodded as the scene was played out for him. "He thought to kill him, and use his magic. Had I not been out looking for those herbs you sent me for, Raven, he would have finished his task. He has only just left here."

"The poison can be worked out of his system, but he will need something to make him sicker." Kenton asked if human things would work. "I think so. For him being as large as he is, he still has a stomach, but we will need a great deal more than for a human."

They worked for twenty minutes on making a batch of medicine to make the dragon throw up more. The magic that had been used on Darmor was man made, something that had been fed to him. Darmor didn't have any trouble swallowing the brew down, and nearly as soon as it hit his belly, it came up with a gush.

Several times over the next hour Darmor was fed the brew, only to have it come right back up. It seemed to be working too. He looked better, and he was no longer as hot as he'd been. Lewis thought a dragon should be hot, but not this one. He was an earth dragon, one that didn't spew forth fire, but helped the

145

earth with warming the ground as well as keeping the trees and animals in the forest safe.

"You're looking much better." Darmor nodded and sat up, leaning against the wall of the cave. "We'll need to get you moved when you think you can. If he found you here, he'll return to finish the job."

"You have a barn for me?" Lewis assured him that he did. "I will stay there. Magic there will keep him from finding me again. You are a kind man, Lord Lewis. I cannot thank you enough for coming to my aid."

"You're very welcome. I've only just gotten my own dragon now, and I'd hate to think of someone trying to hurt me or one of my brothers when we're in that form." Darmor nodded and stood up. When he spread out his wings, Lewis realized what a magnificent creature he really was. "There are others coming. Will they be a grand as you?"

"Yes. Some more, some less, but I will be the biggest." Lewis was actually sort of relieved about that. To hide one dragon this size was going to be tough. Several of them might be impossible.

When Poe led Darmor to their home, Lewis helped Raven gather up the scales that had been left behind. Careful not to break or chip them, he asked her why she didn't handle them on her own. She had him picking them up with a cloth around his hand.

"They're magical. And not only that, but if a female of breeding age touches one, then she will conceive the next time she has sex. It wouldn't matter, either, if they were mates or not. A child would be born." He asked if she was kidding. "No.

Women for centuries would go to a witch that they knew was friends with a dragon. All manner of women, from rich to poor. The coin that would be paid for such a thing was great, too. I don't know that many women use the method now, but back in my day, it was very well known."

"And you're not touching them because you don't want to have a child?" Raven told him that they'd never talked about it. "I see. I guess we've been a little busy. Would you like to have a child? With me?"

Kenton cleared his throat, and they both turned to him. "I don't know about you guys, but I'd not tell Mom about this magic. She'll be cutting it up on every drink or food that any of you ladies partake in. She'll have grandchildren popping out every nine months for sure." They all laughed. "All right, I've contacted Emma, and she's coming for me in the car. I'm to meet her outside. You guys need to talk anyway."

When they were alone, he asked her again about the baby. "I don't want you to make this decision because it will make my mom happy. But I would like to know what your feelings are about them." She nodded, but still didn't touch the scale. "Raven, if you'd rather not have a child, that's fine too. It's your body, and I'd never force you to do anything that you'd not be one hundred percent on board with."

"I don't know that I'd like a child right now." He nodded. "With my lack of sight and the fact that I'd be handicapped in keeping them safe if Butler came for them, I'd never forgive myself if something happened to them. Or to you. But a child, it would be something that he'd take, and I'd do anything for him to get it back. Not that I'd trust him again, but I'd not hesitate

147

to try."

"I understand that. I really do." He picked up two more pieces of the precious magic and put them into the bag she always wore. "I think I'd like one of those bags. I can't imagine what you have in that thing, but it seems to be able to hold a great deal."

"You've changed the subject. Does that mean that you're upset with me or willing to wait?" He pulled her into his arms after putting the last of the scales into the bag. "Lewis, I'd never be able to live with myself if our child got hurt."

"I know that. God, I know that. And you are perfectly right...he'd take our child, and any one of us would do just what he said to get it back. I promise you, I'm not upset at all at your decision. I think it's a good solid reason for waiting." She asked him if he was sure. "I've never been as sure about something as I am of this. But someday, and I'm hoping that it will be sooner rather than later, I hope we do have many children together. And that they have children too. And so on and so on."

They held hands on their way back to the house. He also managed to find the herbs that she wanted. Well, she found them, and he pulled them for her. There was so much in the forest that could be used for so many things, and he loved every minute that he got to spend with Raven finding them.

Going to work later that night, he was getting the meal prepped when his assistant Patty came to talk to him. She had been promoted last night after all the dinners had been served and the place cleaned up. She had been right. There hadn't been a single complaint, nor had anyone gotten upset at the wait they sometimes had.

"We are booked for tonight as well." Lewis wasn't going to freak out again, he told himself. "But I do have a request from someone. They want to know if you could cater a wedding."

"I don't know; can we?" Patty grinned. "I don't know if you're aware of this or not, but that grin of yours, it's not terribly comforting right now."

"Dinner for two hundred guests. No serving, but a buffet line. I've already looked into a couple of places we can get hot services, as well as larger trays. My husband, he's a bartender for one of the bars in the next town over, and he said he'd help us out with it." Lewis just listened to her, knowing that she would have all the details worked out before coming to him. "Flowers are going to be done by the bride's parents. Liquor is also going to be paid for by them. The venue is going to be the large building on Tenth, the one that looks like a big barn."

"It was a dance hall at one time, I think." She said that it was. "And they're okay with using a barn for this thing? You know, I think I might own that building too."

"You do. And once it gets out that you have a large venue for things like weddings and graduation parties, you'll have to hire more crew to run that part, and another assistant." He told her that would be her department. "You mean hiring someone?"

"No, the barn. You take it over and tell me what you need to make it work. You have a good head on your shoulders." She stared at him for several seconds, and Lewis closed her mouth for her. "Congratulations, you're a party planner."

"Seriously? You want me to run that and here too?" He told

149

her if she thought she could handle both, then yes. But if not, to hire her a staff. "You're not kidding, are you?"

"No. I don't joke about my job." She laughed, then did a little dance around the room. He knew that she'd make it work. Patty was very good at organizing and putting all her ducks in a row. "Also, if you think you can work with him full time, I want you to hire your husband for me. I need a good bartender here, and he can work the barn with you when you need him."

"How much can I pay him? I mean, he'd have to make at least what he's making now, or we couldn't afford it." Lewis told her to double his salary and hers. "Lewis, that's a lot of money. You're already paying me more than I thought I'd be making as a hostess."

"I know what your worth is, and so should you." He thought about how much more she'd be working, as would he. "You'll need a staff that is all your own. And I'll need more workers here. A chef, too, that can take over should I need the time off. And we'll need to...you know what? Come to my house for dinner tomorrow night and we'll work out the details. But as of right now, you're making more money, and bring your husband. We'll get this worked out."

Patty was dancing around the room again when the first order came in. She'd been training someone to help her at the hostess station since last night, so that was going to have to double up as well. Christ, he'd just taken on more work than he'd thought possible, and was happy for it.

By the time dinner was over for them, he'd made a list of things that he wanted to figure out. The kind of food that would be served at the barn. A name for it as well. Then there was the liquor license he was going to need to extend, and a few hundred other things that he was sure he was missing. He was just cleaning up the grill when he thought of a name for the place. The next time Patty came back to tell him something, he put it to her.

"How about we call it Caelin's Dream?" She asked him why that name. "It's the name of a friend of mine, and it means powerful warrior. What do you think?"

"I love it. Dragons are powerful, so I can understand the connection to the two. Dragons Lair and Caelin's Dream. I think it's perfect." He did as well, and told her that they would need a logo. "Yes, a dragon for sure. To keep up with the theme of this place."

By the time Lewis was home again, it was nearly midnight. He might have been home sooner, but he was talking to Patty and forgot the time. But as soon as he was in his bedroom, trying his best to be quiet, Raven tossed the blanket off herself, and he nearly fell getting out of his pants.

"Come here, big boy, and show me a good time." He laughed when she did, and joined her. "I love you, Lewis. So very much."

~~~

Raven wanted to be sexy. She had no idea how to be anything but herself, but she was going to give it her best shot. The bed shifted when Lewis joined her, and reaching for him made her heart beat a little faster. When he took her into his arms, she felt his thick hard cock brush against her leg.

"This is what a man likes to come to bed to...a warm, beautiful woman that's all his." Rolling him to his back, she sat over him. His cock was between her thighs, so she reached down and curled her fingers around him. "Baby, if you keep that up, I'm not going to last very long."

"Honestly, I don't care how long you last. I need this." He helped her settle over him, but didn't touch her. "Lewis, if I come like this, will you come with me? Later, I mean?"

"Yes, anything you want. You do what you need, and I'll watch. I love watching you come all over me. And the way that your nipples tighten just perfectly for me." He touched his mouth to one. Moaning at the feel of his mouth so close made her pussy swell too. "I can smell you, Raven. You're so hot and wet for me."

His fingers brushed over her clit, and she cried out with a short release. Begging him to do it again, Raven came twice more when he touched her gently. But it wasn't enough. And when she tried to get him to help her, he told her that he didn't want to take over.

"If you don't take me, I'm going to put a spell on your dick and make it hard all the time. How will you explain that to your mom?" She was suddenly on her back and him over her. His cock didn't just fill her, but seemed a very hard part of her. "Take me. Please. I need to come in the worst kind of way."

"I think that you should suffer." Slapping him on the shoulder made him move again. When he filled her a second time, she cried out. "Yes, suffering sounds good. I was so excited to see you coming, and now I have to do all the work on my own."

"You're a bastard." When he laughed, she knew that he really was going to make her suffer. But as soon as he moved again, slamming his cock deeper into her, she held on for the ride of her life.

"Come for me baby." She screamed when he bit down on her throat. There wasn't that much pain, but it was wonderfully erotic. And when he suckled hard on the wound, she felt like he was touching every part of her heart. Coming a second time was almost too much, but he wasn't done yet.

He touched her everywhere. Her elbows, her nose. Even him touching the back of her neck, which was normally not so tender, made her wetter and needier. His mouth brushed over her chin, her forehead, and her fingers. Every time he licked a part of her, just tasting her flesh, she knew that he was building up for something, making her need higher than it had ever been before.

"Your skin is like the ocean. Soft and beautiful, as well as strong and resilient. Your breath on my skin is like the dragon's breath, warm and comforting, and just as hot." He moved over her, his cock still deep inside of her as he touched his mouth to her ribs and his hands to her ass. "I love the way you respond to me. The way you pink up when you're excited. And when you come, screaming out your release, it's like an arrow to my heart. I fall more in love with you every time."

"Lewis, please. You're killing me." He laughed gently and told her that he loved touching her. "Yes, but you're not letting me come. I can feel it right there, but I can touch it."

He told her to wrap her legs around him. That didn't help at all…he was not giving her what she needed. But when he moved, his body taking and giving her his, she held onto him, and dug her heels into his flesh as he took her higher and higher with each stroke.

For several seconds her heart stopped beating, her body poised on the edge of a cavern. And when she fell, falling over the edge and more in love with Lewis, the world blinked into focus for her. Darkness was her lifelong friend, but in that split second, she saw him there…Lewis was holding her as he took his own pleasure. Then she let the darkness take her once again, sadder because she'd gotten a glimpse of seeing once again.

The sun was filling the room when she woke. Raven looked around the room several times before she realized what she was seeing. Everything. The room was there for her to see. Screaming for Lewis, she laughed when he came out of the bathroom with a towel falling off the hips of his great dragon.

"You're beautiful." He was still looking around the room and she laughed at him. What a sight to see…a dragon with shaving cream on his face, a tiny looking razor in his hand, and his spikes up all along his back.

The walls around him shattered, the floor under his large claws buckled and broke. He had a bit of glass on his shoulder, and a little of the shower curtain seemed to be stuck on one of his spikes. And to her, he was the most beautiful, handsome thing in the world.

"I can see you, Lewis. I can see you in all your glory. I can really see you. Come to me…I want to touch you too."

The dragon stared at her for several minutes. He didn't speak, but when Lewis took his body back, he came to the bed with her. He didn't touch her, but just stared at her face, her eyes, as if he was trying to see for himself if she was joking or not.

"Can you really see me?" Raven nodded. "What color are my eyes? And my hair. What color were my wings"

"Blue, blond, and sapphire. The chair by the fireplace is green. The pillow on it is paisley. Your towel that you dropped is also green—I love the color, by the way—and the blanket over me is also paisley, but much calmer than the pillow. Did you pick this out?" He nodded, then shook his head. "I don't understand."

"It was what matched the chair when you sat in it at the furniture store when we were there. I just got whatever went with it so that it would look good." When he touched his fingers to her face, Raven leaned into his palm and told him she loved him. "And I love you. Please tell me that sex didn't fix your sight."

She laughed hard with that, hard enough that she had to have tissues to stem the tears. Twice she tried to tell him that she thought it was a gift from Caelin, but she kept laughing at the expression on his face. Lewis was trying his best not to laugh too, but finally he gave in. He held her while she told him what had transpired between the two of them, her and Caelin, the night of his grand opening.

"He told me that he had a gift for me. I told him that he'd given me so much already, or something like that. I had no idea this was what he meant." Lewis still wasn't saying much, but she didn't care. "I can see now. I can't believe it. The colors are so.... Everything is so bright and colorful. After all.... We have to go outside. I want to see the grass and trees."

"All right." They were both dressed in seconds. He had to go back and finish shaving, and she stood beside him watching.

It was all new to her. Not just the colors, but the mirrors, the tile in the bathroom. Even the pictures on the wall. "You keep staring at me like that and I'll more than likely cut my face."

"I'm sorry, but you have no idea what this feels like. I was in darkness...every part of the world and things in it were taken from me. I missed so much. And now, it's like I have been given it all back, and it's almost too much." She kissed him on his shoulder and sat on the toilet to wait for him. "I don't want to miss a thing. You know, in case this is just a one-day thing. I want to see it all and savor it."

Lewis finished up quickly, then took her out to the yard. Raven danced around the yard several times, just laughing and pointing at different things. The pigs had arrived, and she went to see them. The unicorn welcomed her with a butting of her head. Raven could not get enough of anything.

"You must think me mad." Lewis told her no, he thought she was perfect. "I'm far from that, but I don't think I could be happier than I am right at this moment. I must thank Caelin. He did this for us."

"He did, and I have to thank him too, for making you this happy." She went to sit by him on the deck. Holding him like she was, Raven touched the fabric of his pants, the wood that was their home. "The trees will be turning soon. You'll be able to see that as well. And then snow falling. Even the tree that we'll put up in the house, you will be able to marvel at it too."

"Are you making fun of me?" He said that he would never do anything like that, but was just thinking of what she could see. "Yes. I've never seen a tree decorated. My mother, we didn't do things like that. There wasn't usually enough money for things for the holidays. We would exchange a gift, but never a tree. And snow. I love the snow, and how it cleans everything and makes it ready for the freshness of the spring. I hope this isn't a one-day thing, Lewis. I will be heartbroken if it is."

"I can't see him doing that to anyone. He wouldn't to you, especially." She nodded and watched a blue jay go to the feeder and scare the smaller birds away. "Besides, if this is a cruel joke, I'll make sure that he remembers that we're dragons too. He'll fix it."

"You're my big, strong hero." They were laughing when entering the house. There, sitting on the table, was a large vase of orchids, of every color imaginable, and the note with it was addressed to her.

I love you, my child. And the sight that you now enjoy will be yours forever. Never again will you have to pay the price for your magic. This to you I swear. I love you both, Caelin.

Raven asked if they could go out to breakfast, because she wanted to see the town. And of course, Lewis told her that he wanted to see his mom and let her know, and Raven was going to get to see them all for the first time. This day was going to be the best one of her life, she decided.

Chapter 11

Butler hated people. Unless they served him in some way, he wanted nothing to do with them. That was why you had servants and people who would do things for you. So that people like him, kings, wouldn't have to mingle with the sub human race. But today he was on a mission. Today, he was going to talk to the McCades.

The streets were busy today. Even though it was late in the afternoon, he thought that some of, if not all, these people needed to be at work, doing something more than socializing. If he were in charge, and he would be soon enough, he'd beat them to death, just to show them what it was like to have a person of worth in charge.

Laughing at his own thinking, he knew that wouldn't work. If he beat them all to death, then who would serve him? No, he'd just make an example of a few of them, and that would be all it took. They'd be bowing before him in a matter of moments.

Butler paused in front of a store front, seeing items there that he'd not seen before.

The sign said that it was a vintage butter churn. The thing looked like it would be better served as a buggy, perhaps to shake up the kid that would cry too much. But there were other items in the window too, all of them with prices on them that made him think that if anyone paid for such items, those prices anyway, then they deserved whatever he did to them. Who would pay eight hundred dollars for a chest of drawers made of oak?

"No one in their right fucking mind, that's who." He looked at the woman who huffed at him. "Fuck off, my dear. I'm allowed to have my own opinion, and I'll say what I wish when I wish."

"Yes, you can, but I would appreciate it if you'd curb your language while having your opinion. What if there had been a child about?" He looked around and saw that there were a great many children running up and down the streets, and sidewalks too. "They hear it enough, they don't need strangers saying it as well."

"Fuck you." He knew the moment that she glared that he had gone too far. The cane that she had in her hand was suddenly at his forehead and banging him hard. Before he could get away from her, he tripped on his own feet and went down.

The bitch never stopped hitting him with it. When she started away, his head and nose bloodied, she leaned down to him and said, in a voice as clear as rain, "Fuck you too."

What was this world coming to? Women no longer knew

their station. They said and did what they wanted, no matter that a man was much smarter and stronger. He looked in the direction that the old biddy had gone and cursed her again, but he did do it quietly this time. There was no sense in him getting knocked around again.

Turning to go the way he'd been headed, he saw a woman walking on the other side of the street. There was something very familiar about her. A man was with her, holding her hand like she was something special to him. Women were responsible for that, a man being so sappy that they didn't pay any attention to what was right.

When she laughed, Butler knew the sound. Moving to follow the couple, he tried to think who it might be, where he'd seen her. As he got closer to them, the man stopped and so did the woman. It wasn't until the man turned and looked at him that Butler felt like the world was slipping under his feet.

"Caelin?" The man looked so much like his son that it took his breath away. He was taller, and seemed to be just a little.... He wasn't sure what it was, but he was more than his son was. Magical? Perhaps, but there was something for him to be frightened of. "I'm sorry. I have the wrong —"

"Hello, Butler." The woman spoke to him without his permission. When he drew back his hand to slap her, his feeling still reeling from the man, she laughed again. "You do, and this will end badly for you."

"Who do you think you are, talking to me as if I know you? And it's King Butler, not...." Then it hit him who she was. "Raven of the Wood? You're her, the witch that tricked me?"

"Nay, I did nothing of the sort, but you look like a man

161

down on his luck. Have you had some troubles of late? Do you, perhaps, know that this is the end for you, and have given up all hope?" The man with her laughed, but said nothing. How could he do that, he wondered, and stared at him again. "This is my husband, Lewis McCade."

He did fall back then, hitting his ass on the sidewalk as she and the man, a fucking McCade, stood over him, laughing. Several things clicked in his head then. The fact that she was still alive. That she could see him. That the fucking bitch was married to a McCade.

"You will come with me, Raven of the Wood. I have a need for your magic." She looked at McCade, and he wondered if he knew what he was married to. "She is a witch; did you know that? A dark witch that works with the devil himself. She isn't to be trusted. Give her over to me and I'll not bother you for the rest of the day."

"You'll not bother either of us for the rest of our lives. And from what I'm to understand, you don't have too much longer for your own life, do you?" McCade bent down, his knees just at his face, and smiled at him. "You touch anyone in my family, and I will gladly start this mess over just to see you dead. Mark my words, Butler, I am a man who can and will kill you where you stand."

"You think I'm afraid of you?" McCade nodded and stood up, wrapping his arms around Raven of the Wood. "You are wrong, my boy. And when I get the pieces from you and your family, I will cut them from your women like they are nothing but trash, as they are."

"You think so? I don't. I think what is going to happen is,

you're going to die by our hand, and we'll all live very long and very happy lives knowing that you're not a part of them." When they turned their back to him, he got up. It was difficult for him, being in so much pain. He reached for the man, but before he could touch him, he turned again. "Touch me and I'll rip your arm from your body and beat you to death with it."

The words were said in a calm, low voice. There was no screaming at him, no knife or gun pointed when he said it. His voice never rose as Butler's might have. The man's threat—nay, his promise—was said in a way that Butler believed him. Not just believed, but feared that he would follow through with it even if he didn't touch him.

Butler was still standing there, his hand outstretched, when he realized he was alone. They were both gone. He could see nothing of them, and wondered how long they'd been standing there. Putting his hand in his pocket, to hold onto his aching belly, he moved toward the outskirts of town to the place he'd been calling home for the last few days.

He needed to think. To plan and to go over what Raven of the Wood would mean to his plans. There was so much riding on this, too much for him to lose sight of the import of her being there.

Raven was a powerful witch. And over the decades, he knew that she could only have become stronger. That should have been something that he'd thought of, he knew now. When he couldn't find her, he should have known that she'd be hiding, and it wasn't her hiding herself; Caelin had been hiding her for his offspring. The circle, it was closing up on him.

He'd known this day was coming since he'd married his

wife, Prisane, and started to do things that were better suited for himself. Butler never loved her and didn't even like her, but she had money and station, and he wanted that. And a son to train in the ways of himself.

Greedy? Yes, he was that and more. A bastard? He supposed he was that as well. The son of a woman who had no husband other than the men that she brought to the house to pay her. He ate well, until she started to lose her looks. By then, he'd managed to make himself into the man he was today. A materialistic bastard that took what he wanted and killed whoever gainsaid him.

Butler hadn't really believed the tales that were told to him. His wife was powerful, yes, but without a man to tell her what to do, she was nothing more than fluff. Or so he'd thought. Now he knew that she was solely responsible for him having no other sons. And in a way, the murder of all the women who had given him nothing but females as offspring.

The jewelry too. She'd been the one that had kept him from it, and the monies that should've rightfully been his. Almost as soon as he'd touched the necklace that now hung around his neck, the castle had started to fall. He and his men, they'd barely gotten out with their lives when he'd wrapped the heavy thing around the neck of his new wife.

"And searching the area never turned up anything. Not a coin to call my own. Not a single painting that I'd not stolen. The barns, still standing, had nary a horse or nag in them." He sat on the falling down porch of his home and thought of how many times he'd been there, gone back to find where she had hidden his things. "It's like she had put them under a spell too, and stolen them from my hands."

Butler took many wives after that, and women who were close enough for him to fuck. It mattered little to him if they were maiden or old. And if they had already birthed a son, he'd tie them to his bed and fuck them daily until they were fat with a child. But no matter who he took, no matter the children they had birthed before, he never once sired a son but the one with Prisane.

He pulled the necklace out of his shirt and looked at it. It held no magic for him. He could only see a pasty white jewel among others of equal ugliness. The clasp that held it together had long since been broken, and he'd had to tie a string to it to fit around his large neck.

Legend said that with a bit of magic, you could see its worth. He'd never seen anything but the way it looked to him now. Worthless to anyone that gazed upon it that didn't know that it held a magic that would rule the world. And he would. As soon as he had the other pieces.

But, and this was the real kicker, he didn't have any idea how to draw the dragon out. What he was supposed to do to command it. Nor did he know if there was a saying he had to say, or when to say it. The prophecy said that when the time came, when all the family, mates, and dragons were together, then the dragon within would tell them how to bring it forth, and all the riches.

So while he did threaten to kill them off, the women, he knew that in this, they were important for him to get what he wanted. Then he'd have no trouble killing them all and being done with this whole thing.

"But where are the dragons?" He remembered the one that he'd trapped in the cave, and decided to go see to him now. "He should be about gone, and I can take what I need from him."

His habit of talking to himself had started long ago. Mostly when he was thinking about his plans, he'd toss around ideas like they were pieces of paper. Not that he could read or write, but talking his way through them had been his way of getting where he was now. On top of the world, as far as he was concerned.

The cave was deep, and he wished, like he had the first time, that he'd remembered to bring himself a torch. A flashlight, he thought they were called now. A tiny little thing that could give off more light than a sun in a dark room. Laughing at the silliness of that, he trudged on.

When he'd been searching for over an hour, by his estimation, Butler believed that he'd made a couple of wrong turns when he finally realized the dragon was simply gone. Going to the mouth of the cave to start again, he knew that he was correct. Someone had taken his dragon. When he sat upon a large stone, one that he was going to use as a cutting surface, a light shown against the wall, startling him.

"Hello, dumbass." He looked around and wondered who this man was talking to. "You, you moron. I'm talking to you. I had no idea that I could do this, so listen up, bud. I took Darmor to my home. He is resting well and feeling better all the time. No thanks to you."

"You've no rights to him. He was my dragon." The man laughed, and he thought of the other man, the husband of Raven of the Wood. "Who are you?"

"I am Kenton McCade, king of the dragons that you dared to harm." Butler didn't like this, but didn't let the man know it. "Are you scared? You should be. Wetting your pants kind of scared. But I'm going to give you a little advice. None of us think you're going to heed it, but here it is. Get out. Get far away from here now, because we're coming for you, Butler, bastard son of Mildred the Whore."

Then he was gone, and the little bit of light with him. Butler was afraid. The magic that had been used here, it would have given him so much more than he had now. Standing up, he hit his head on the boulder over his head and fell to the ground. Butler laid there...he had to think.

~~~

Vance sat at his kitchen table and tried to think. There were a lot of things that he could be doing right now, more than just the house he was having worked on, but he needed to get his head together. Having things in turmoil would get him hurt. And Vance thought that he'd been in pain enough for one or two lifetimes.

His mate was coming here. She'd just show up, he'd been told. Someone was guiding her, he knew that, but she could be one of millions of women out there. None of them, he thought, would want to be his mate. Not forever, as he was going to be living.

The checklist he had in front of him wasn't written in any language that his family could read. Sanskrit had been a language that he'd picked up easily enough, out of necessity really, and he'd been using it since for his own personal use. Making lists was something that he did all the time, but only

167

when he was home. Other times, like on the job, he never wrote a thing down. Nor did he email anyone, leave phone messages, or even make a grocery list. Vance was always careful.

The men that were working on his home were people that he trusted. Two men...in all his life, he'd trusted only two men other than his own brothers, and now their wives. When Samuel came and sat across from him, he laid his gun on the table between them.

"You gonna use that on me, buddy?" Vance shook his head. "You don't plan on using it on yourself, do you? I can't let you do that, Vance. We have a job to do, and I won't have you fucking it up by putting a bullet in your head."

"Won't do me a bit of good. I'm an immortal." Samuel nodded. Vance wasn't sure if he believed him or not, but it didn't matter. "I have a plan. When will you be done here?"

"Couple of days. Not too much more to do other than the security system. State of the art, nothing on the grid. You gonna take care of the paperwork?" He told him it was done. "You thinking you won't come out on the good end of this plan? I mean, if you're immortal, like you said, then you'll be coming back."

"Prison won't be kind to me." No, Samuel said, it would not be. "If we're caught, you know what they'll do to us. A firing squad won't be in our future. They'll hide us so deep and so well that even a vampire won't find us."

"Maybe not, but at least, with what you've done, a great many people might start looking for us. The papers, you thinking they might bury it too? Like the government did?" Vance said they'd not be able to. "What did you do?"

"My brother, he's good with a computer. And my nephew too. They'll make sure that it gets out there." Samuel asked if they'd be hurt. "No, not them. Grady, he'll bounce it enough that no one would ever have it come back on him."

Bouncing off other networks. Spending just enough time at one site for another one to be found. It was a great deal like pool. Hitting the ball and having it go all over the place before you were able to calculate where it was going to fall. Or hoped it would fall.

"Some flunkies have been tracking the movements of us in the circle. Most of them don't have a clue who they're chasing, but they have orders to keep an eye on the ball. Yours are at the top of the list, then mine and the other two. You still don't care about Sawyer?" Vance shook his head. "You still think he's in on it then?"

"He is." Samuel said nothing. Vance wouldn't fill him in on the details, not even if asked. He knew that Sawyer was a part of it, and had been bugged like they were to put off suspicions that he wasn't a part of the group. Why they'd done that, he didn't know, but he would before this was finished.

Plus his friend would help him. Jeff was better at computers than anyone he knew. And the man had a way of connecting things that went well beyond even the government that he worked for. But no one, not even Samuel, would ever know about Jeff. He was his ace in the hole for everything.

"When you are finished up here, we'll leave. My family is having a big to do that night, and I'll be there. You pack light and I'll meet you at the car." Samuel said that he'd be there. "There will be no coming back from this. If you want out you

169

tell me now, and no one will ever be the wiser."

"They stuck these fuckers in my body without telling me. And the fact that I didn't have any say or anything to do with it pisses me off." Vance said nothing again. "I want them to pay, Vance. More than you do. They've set me up. Taken away my freedom even when I'm on rest and relax. That shit don't fly with me."

After he left, Vance continued to sit at his table. Making a mental note to mark that off his list, he wasn't surprised when Sawyer entered the house and sat with him. He was a nosey Gus, as his mom would say, and hated when he didn't have all the information that Vance did. But since Vance had figured it out, he knew why now.

"Having some work done on your house, Vance? I didn't even know you had one until I saw it in the papers that you'd gotten yourself one." Vance asked him what he was doing looking up houses for him. "I wasn't. Just curious. What sort of shit you got going on here? Looks like you got yourself a new kitchen and shit. I don't cook, do you?"

"I'm leaving. And I want you to forget my address. We're not friends." Sawyer nodded but didn't move. Vance picked up his gun and aimlessly aimed at him. "You come back here, Sawyer, and that will be the last time you come here. Got it?"

"Yeah, got it. Why are you so testy all the time? I'm just trying to be friendly. You and Sam, you guys are the hardest people in the world to get to know." Vance stood up and let himself go a little. He didn't have his dragon, but he was a big man. "You trying to impress me, buddy? I don't swing that way, just so you know."

"You swing anyway the wind blows, and we both know it." He leaned down to face the man, hatred seeming to boil off him at that moment. "Get out of my house, and don't you fucking return."

When he was gone, Vance wandered through the house. Things were about done. Even the furniture that he'd gotten had been inspected for any kind of devices, as well as the linens. Everything was going to be safe, for anyone that lived here.

He didn't figure that he was going to return for long. It would take them a bit to sort things out from the fall out, and he hoped that by then, the woman would show up, he'd sign the house over to her, and the dragon would be called. Vance didn't want his family to suffer for this, but there wasn't going to be any hope for it. The guys in office, including the White House, were dirty. And making a great deal of money off him and his men.

The house, as of now, belonged to him. But if he were to disappear for more than thirty days, after he was gone the last time, it would go to Lewis. Lewis would get a certified letter in the mail telling him what to do, where to send the information, as well as how to contact Jeff. He had covered all his bases, and right now, it was a waiting game.

Three months ago he'd found out that he had trackers in his body. Five of them, as a matter of fact. And the reason for so many was because if he lost a limb or any part of his body, they'd still be able to keep track of where he was. Gruesome, but well planned out.

From then on, he'd been searching for the people that had put them there. Also tracking who else might have them. He'd

171

concluded that he was in deeper shit than he'd first thought, and so were the men that worked with him. Since then, he'd lost three of them, to random acts of violence, and he was sure that Samuel was next. Then it would leave just him and Sawyer.

Joseph Sawyer had gotten under his radar. Not only had he accepted him on his team, but he knew things, like about his family, that Vance wished now he'd not told him. The man was reporting back to the president, as well as the vice president and a couple of others.

The reason he'd been able to figure that out was that he'd given different stories as to what he was going to do for a living after this to each of the men, and Sawyer's was the only one that he'd found in his jacket. A thick file of every little thing there was to know about him and his family. What his mom did, what his brothers did for a living, and the net worth of each of them. It was scary, too, that on a weekly basis, that information changed with the stock market. When they made or lost money, it was reported to someone somewhere and put there. They were watching him better than his mom did, he thought.

You have a minute? He told Lewis that he was just going over his house again. *Yeah, about that. Did you send someone to my house to check on security?*

No. Is it a wiener looking kid that needs a shave? He said it was. *His name is Sawyer. And he's been warned. Do whatever you want with him because if I see him, he's dead.*

When Lewis laughed, Vance smiled. Whatever he'd said or done to the man, it seemed to have tickled him a bit. Vance was on his way to his brother's house when Raven spoke to him. She too was laughing.

If this guy comes up missing, will anyone care? I doubt even his mother would. He told her about the trackers in his body. *I'm not worried about those. But I think this guy just pissed himself. Poe met him at the door and spoke to him. The guy took off running from here like he'd been shot from a gun. Funniest thing I've seen in a while.*

Vance was still laughing when he got into his truck. Making his way to Lewis's home, he got a run down on the happenings of Sawyer. Seeing the man on the road as he drove over, he thought seriously about just running him down, but didn't. That would have messed up his day. But it was funny to see him running away, screaming over his shoulder about birds that talked and cursed at you. Vance wished he had a video of that…it would have made for some good times while he was in prison.

His family was already at his mom's when they pulled up. He had picked up Lewis and Raven, and they were still laughing about Sawyer. Mom came out of the house to greet them, as she always did, but he knew she had something on her mind. When the other two went inside, he looked down at the most important woman in his life. His mom was his world.

"You're leaving soon, aren't you?" He just kissed her on the forehead. "Vance, when are you going to come home for good? I miss you while you're away. And since I haven't any idea where you are, every time something comes on the news, I wonder if I'm going to get a call from someone."

"There won't be any calls from anyone if I'm hurt, Mom." She asked him why not. "I don't exist anymore. Not to any agency or group." She stared at him for several moments, and he hugged her. "I promise you, I take as much care of myself as

173

I can. I won't come to you in a box."

"That's not very comforting, Vance. You know that, don't you?" Vance told her it was the best he could do. "I love you, son. I wish you'd come home."

"I will, as soon as this last thing is over with." She nodded, but didn't look convinced. "Mom, I can't tell you anything, but I will promise you that as soon as this is over, I'll be done."

"Done how?" He didn't answer her again. "I see. And when you're done, will I only be able to visit you in prison, or will there be someplace else that they'll take you?"

"If I play my cards right, I'll be here. If not, there is no prison for me. They'll bury me." She nodded and held him tighter to her. "I love you, Mom. And when she gets here, please take care that my mate is safe. Until I return, or you'll know what happened."

"I promise you that, but you come back to me, and her. You come back here and tell me all about it." Vance nodded. "Good. I suppose that's the best I can hope for in this."

Vance was going to make sure that his mom never knew what he'd been up to these last years. It was too much for him at times; it would break his mom's heart even if she knew only about half of what he'd been doing. Going into the house for dinner, Vance was as happy as the rest of them that Raven had gotten her sight back. It was a day for celebrating, and he was glad to be there.

Chapter 12

Raven made her way to the barn, but was thinking of all the things that she had to take care of today. The doors were closed up; a spell would keep anyone from going in, but there was something off about it that had her pausing in mid step and waiting for Poe.

"I see a little bit of magic." She told him that she could see it as well. "I can go into the barn from the top…I have put in an opening just for me. Check it out and let you know."

His voice, usually at the top of the spectrum when he spoke, was low, like her own. When she told him to go but to be careful, he flew off her shoulder and to the top of the big barn. After waiting a few minutes, not only did the donkeys come out of the door, but the unicorn as well.

There is a disturbance, my lady, but nothing to worry over. Asking him what it was, he laughed. *It seems that our goats have decided that they want to be parents as well. The magic that came*

175

from them being transported has given them a boost to have children. Come see them. They have a pair of kids.

Hurrying now, she entered the barn just as the donkeys joined them. The goats were in the back of the barn near the window when she found them. They were the most adorable things she'd ever seen. Asking for permission to hold them, she was delighted to see that there was one of each, a black one and a brown one as well as male and female. Raven asked the proud parents what they wanted to name them.

"All right then, Ann and Drew. I love those names, by the way." She played with them a little more, amazed at how soft they were and that she could actually see them. When she was ready to go to the field to find some herbs she wanted in her gardens, she turned in time to see a man with a gun to Aisha's head. Her temper nearly got the better of her when she paused to figure out what was going on. Leaping head first into this was going to get someone hurt.

When she said Aisha's name, they both turned toward her, and she could see that it was the man from yesterday. Poe landed on the ground in front of her and told the man to let her go. Of course, he shot at her pet and Poe took off.

"What the fuck do you think you're doing?" Sawyer said he wanted to know where Vance was. "How the hell should I know? I'm not his keeper. But you've fucked up badly now. That's my mother-in-law you have there, and I'm going to kill you."

"I tried reasoning with him, dear, but he just wasn't having it. I told him, several times as a matter of fact, that my sons were going to hurt him badly, but he only hit me with that fool gun

LEWIS

of his. I would have shot him myself, but he got the jump—"
Sawyer told Aisha to shut up. "Listen up, young man. I will not
be spoken to like that. You unhand me this minute or else."

"Or else what? You're an old woman, and she's way over
there. And that bird...I don't know how you did that, but I'm
not afraid now. Not that I was before, but he startled me. Yes,
that's it, I was startled." Aisha laughed when she did. "This
isn't funny. Tell me where Vance and that other man are, and
I'll let you go."

"You think that Vance is going to be happy that you've hurt
his mother? If I don't kill you, he most assuredly will. And not
easily either." Sawyer told her to shut up too. "My goodness,
you are going to be so dead. You just wait. I'm betting by
nightfall, you're not only going to be pissing blood from a lot of
holes in you, but in the morgue doing it too."

"Vance left without me. We're partners, and we're going
on a mission together." Raven said nothing, but did search the
man's mind. She had asked last night if she could do that when
he showed up again, and Vance told her to have at it. "I want
you to tell me where he is, or there will be hell to pay."

"You mean from your bosses? I guess when you're in as
deep as you are, you have to do all sorts of things, don't you,
Joey?" He asked her what she was talking about. "Gambling,
for one thing. And the fact that you've mortgaged your parents'
home to pay some of your debt. What do you think they're
going to do when they find out? Surely not welcome you with
open arms, will they?"

"You don't know what you're talking about." He looked
around, as if expecting someone to come out and help him.

177

"Where did you get that information? From Vance? He doesn't know shit. I'm working to pay it back."

"To who?" She couldn't get a grip on the names that were floating around in his head. He was too stressed out, his mind a jumble of thoughts and rules. "What do you think they're going to say to you when they find out you've broken your cover? They're not going to be happy with you, are they?"

Moving as close to him as she could without alerting him, she kept searching while she spoke. There wasn't any way that she was going to get much, not with his mind like it was, but one thing that she did know...he knew it was only a matter of time before Vance and Samuel found out. That was information that she could work with.

But before she could say anything, even if she had known what to say, the police pulled up. He had his gun out and pointed at them when she saw Vance coming up behind him. When Joey turned toward the sound, she nearly rushed him when Vance spoke to the officer.

"You left me." Vance said nothing, but continued to talk to the cop when Sawyer screamed at him. Whatever they were discussing, the cop seemed hesitant about it. Joey yelled at Vance to tell him where he'd been. "You are supposed to have taken me with you. That isn't the way partners work. What are you doing now?"

The officer handed the rifle out of his car to Vance. She knew what was going to happen the moment Vance put the gun to his shoulder and aimed it at Joey. The man had this coming, but she didn't want anyone to be hurt. Looking at Aisha, she spoke to her through a link.

Don't move. He won't hurt you, but don't move. She said she was pissed off. *Yes, so am I, but this is going to be a good thing. A problem that Vance needed taken care of for his mission.*

You mean he told this man to.... No, he'd not do that. Not Vance. Raven nodded. *He's going to kill him, isn't he?*

The shot rang out, and it was a full second before Joey's head snapped back. Going to Aisha, she held her in her arms when Joey fell back. It was over in a matter of seconds, and the problem was taken care of for a lot of people.

The other brothers showed up just as the ambulance did. Raven wasn't sure, but she thought they'd been told to stand back and to let Vance take care of this. He would have been her choice too in having to kill the man. The amount of concentration and precision to kill a man that far away who was holding his mom would have taken a pro. And Raven was positive that Vance was that and more.

The Army personnel showed up just as Vance was being questioned. There was no doubt that he was going to be in trouble for this. The police were there, and had backed up every word that he said. Even her and her mother-in-law had told them what had happened three times before they finally took the cuffs off him. Vance was told he could go home, but not to leave the state if he knew what was good for him.

Of course, Aisha had something to say about that too. "You are treating him like he's the one that had a gun to my head. The person that came into my house while I was having a lovely cup of tea and a warm scone is dead because my son came here and saved me. Joey, or whatever his name was, he broke my favorite tea cup and hit me with that gun." When

179

the man in the uniform called her ma'am, like he was going to female-splain things to her, Aisha lost her tight control on her emotions. "You try and sweep me under the rug and I will wrap you up in it and bury you in the back yard. That man tried to kill me. He threatened my family. He hurt me, and he took me hostage. And all you have to say to my son, who saved me when you couldn't, is for him not to leave town. I should beat your ass, that's what I should do. The nerve of some people…. He hit me with that gun he had pointed at my head."

"Mrs. McCade, perhaps I can help you with this." Raven could almost taste the man's hatred. Not at them, but at Vance. She didn't know who he was, not really, but he was talking to Aisha about saving the country and the stress of it. "And if you'll allow me to, I'll have a set of the White House china sent to you as my gift for all that you've gone through."

The president. She knew his face, somewhat, but had only seen it in newspapers that she didn't read much, and blurbs on television. Raven looked at Vance as the president went on to explain how they'd had their eyes on Sawyer for some time now, and they were very sorry that it had come to this. Then he assured her that Vance was in no more trouble than she was, and left it at that.

As they sorted through the information, she stood by Lewis. He didn't say anything to them, but did tell the police that he'd arrived after the man was dead. The body camera on the police officer was reviewed, and for a moment, came up missing. Raven *found* it in the pocket of one of the agents. They were trying their best to make it look like a murder, and that Vance had killed that man for no other reason than that he could.

"I'll hold onto this for you until the police take it for evidence. I can't believe that you'd not think about it being in your pocket. You can't just take things like that, I'm sure you know that, don't you?" The agent looked over her head, and she knew that the president was right behind her. "If you need a copy of it, I'm sure that the local police can fix that up for you. It would be no trouble at all."

"I need the original." She told him that wasn't happening. This was a domestic call. "No, we were involved because he was an Army soldier."

"Really? Well, let me give it back to you then." She handed him a different thumb drive that she'd conjured and backed away from him. "I'm really sorry about the confusion there. I thought that since it happened to just regular people like us, that the police would need it more. I don't want anyone to come back later and say that Vance did anything wrong."

Again with the look, but Raven didn't care. Going back to Lewis, she handed him the drive and he slipped it into his pocket. She hadn't any idea if what she said would happen, but Raven wasn't taking any chances in this. Vance had killed a man, justifiably, and she was going to make sure that no one thought differently.

Raven touched the hand of every officer there, each of the agents, and had even managed to shake hands with the president. Each time she did so, she took a little from them, enough to know their thoughts and actions for the rest of their lives. Then she pushed them into telling the truth whenever it came up about this shooting. Even the president would not be able to lie to anyone as to what happened here today.

181

The body was photographed and wrapped up. The ambulance that had come for him was told to stand down. His body was now the property of the government. Again Raven interceded for the family, and was told again that this was a government crime scene. But she used her magic and took the pictures from the camera, and made copies of them by sending them to an online printer. She was quite proud of herself. There would be enough evidence, should anyone try anything, to get them out of hot water. Or at least she hoped so.

By the time everyone had cleared out, and Aisha's address given was to the president for the cups and such, they made their way into their home. Raven was glad that they'd hired someone to cook on the days that Lewis was working, or they might have been eating cereal. Today, she thought, had ended well, but she worried for the future. Butler would be coming, and he'd be taking no prisoners this time.

~~~

"Remind me never to try and pull something over on you." Vance looked at the photos that had spewed out of the printer as soon as they came into Lewis's house. "These are even marked with the file number that the Bureau uses. Do I even want to know how you did this?"

"I can tell you. I've been around for a very long time, and I've learned not to trust people in office, nor to believe anything that anyone with a uniform on says. They tend to cover their own asses before anyone else's." They all laughed, and Lewis handed him the thumb drive. "That's the body cam of the officer. What they have is blank. Well, not blank, but full of static. That way they'll think that they messed it up and that I didn't pull a fast one on them. I was having a great deal of fun too."

"I bet you were." Vance leaned back in the chair and looked around the table. He knew that he had to explain a few things to them, but just where to start, he hadn't any idea. "Sawyer worked for the president. They're trying to keep me under control."

His mom huffed. "I've been trying to do that since you climbed out of your crib when you were six months old. The things that you could get into and out of still amaze me. And if they think that they can do that, then they don't know you very well, do they?" He nodded and told her they thought they did. "I'm sure they think a lot of things. Like, I'm supposing that they think that you killed that man, not because he was holding a gun to my head, but because you knew that he was in on something that they don't think you know about."

"Pretty much." He laughed. "I never could hide anything from you, Mom. How did I ever miss that about you? You're very smart."

"I had to be smart, or I would never have survived raising six boys by myself and trying to keep a rein on the goings on between you six." She patted him on the cheek. "That man, the president, he just happened to be that close when there was trouble with one of his men, as he called them? I don't believe that for a moment. Something else was going on, and he was here for that. Are you in trouble, Vance?"

"Yes, Mom, I'm in a lot of trouble. But I'm working on it." She told him she'd help. "I know you would, but at this point, you can't. None of you can."

183

He told them what he could, which wasn't much. Vance explained that he had the trackers in his body and what they were doing about them. He mentioned that there were only two of them left, two men that they had tagged, and he was sure that Sawyer was going to be next to be killed. And why.

"We came upon a mission that wasn't right. The five of us, my men, came to a town that was supposed to be overrun by the bad guys. But what we found was a peaceful little burg that didn't seem like it had come to the twenty-first century. It was quaint; there were people walking around like they were on holiday. Things like skis on their shoulders, fake snow on the mountain regions. Everyone was friendly, almost too friendly. In one part of town there was a restaurant that served pizza, as well as hot dogs and other Americanized food. Then just as we were ready to leave, something popped out at me, and we knew that we were there to be killed."

"What was it?" He told Kenton that he figured out that the houses weren't real, nor were the little shops. "I don't understand."

"They were fronts. The shops were much too small for the buildings they were in. It didn't occur to me, not right away, but once I realized that the size didn't fit the shop, I started looking deeper. And what I found scared me a great deal." He thought about how complacent he'd been until then. "Behind the fronts were people making guns. Enough ammo was being stacked on shelves that would have ended the war. Uniforms were there, American as well as a couple of other countries. As we were trying to figure out what the hell was going on, we get a call that says for us to stand down, to take a breather."

"They told you of a hotel to go to, and that a meal, something big, was going to be served to you that night, right?" He nodded at Emma. "Yeah, Bart did that once. Came in with guns blazing to kill three men. Ended up killing seventeen people, including the owner who was helping him."

Vance thought of the call, and the reaction that he'd gotten when he told them what he'd found. "They were pissed off that we'd gone snooping around. The guy that I spoke to told me that we might as well put our guns to our head, that we were as good as dead. That we'd stumbled into a place no man returned from. Then there was a gunshot; the man I was talking to was killed, I figured out. After that, it was all we could do to get out of there with our asses. I lost two men, and gained Sawyer."

"So it was a ploy to get you killed, and they knew that you were where you were supposed to be because of the trackers and the fact that you called them. But what did you see that had them wanting you dead? There was something, right?" He nodded, but didn't say anything to Dalton. "You can't tell me. Not yet, anyway."

"No, not until this is finished." He sat up and looked around the room. "I want you all to know that there are some very high up people involved in this. And it's not just about the trackers, but looking into this, I've found a whole lot of things going on that is getting men, men and women like me, killed. Not to mention arms deals that are making them millionaires on the country's dime." His mom asked him if he was going to prison. "There is a possibility of that happening, especially if I fail. I'm not planning on it, but I might. And I have people in place that will make sure that when this all goes down, everyone will know why."

"Recordings, paperwork and the like." He nodded at Dalton. "All right. But there has to be something that we can do to help you. And I still have connections in the department. Hell, they all come to me about every little thing. But if you need something, you ask, and I'll try my best to get it to happen."

"I need for people to think that I'm still in town for a few days. A week, if you all can manage it." Raven stood up and Poe came into the room. When he landed on her shoulder, she touched Lewis. And just like that, he was Vance. "Holy Christ."

Standing up, Lewis stood next to his brother. His mom stood as well and walked around the two of them. It was eerie, standing next to a duplicate of himself, but when his mom smiled at him, he knew that this would work.

"He's a bit taller than you. Not so much that anyone would notice. But we can make this work. Now, what else can we do for you? Bake a cake with a file in it? I'm sure that Emma could do that." Vance laughed. It was an odd feeling, having some humor after so long, but he laughed hard. And when Lewis was himself again, he hugged him to him and told him not to get used to it.

"I won't. You stink, by the way." Vance laughed again. He should have known that they'd be there for him, no matter what. "And for the record, I had no idea that she could do that either. That was just freaky."

"What about the trackers? I mean, he can look like you, but there is still the problem of them being in your body." He looked at Gabe when Kenton asked. "You've taken them out, haven't you? Or at least Gabe has."

Vance laid them on the table. There were six that she'd found; the one in his head had given him a major headache for several hours after it had been removed. He would need them eventually, he supposed, in order to have them where he landed. Lewis picked them up and frowned.

"Okay, if she can make me into you. I think we should try to make these. You've already proven that they can't blow when removed. I'm assuming that they have to be together too?" Vance said he thought so, but hadn't wanted to try it out. "Good point. Let me play a minute. Maybe we can figure this out."

Lewis looked at Raven and winked at her. Vance could see that they loved one another, and it gave him a little pang of jealousy when he saw how in love all of them were. He might not ever have that, not if this went to shit. Lewis handed the trackers to his wife and she smiled.

"They're just trackers, right?" He nodded at Raven. "Okay, this should be easy enough. But the problem is, I won't be able to make them so they last very long. A couple of weeks at the most."

"That's more than enough time for me. Once I give you the signal, you can destroy them here and I'll pick them up on the other end. It'll make them a little wiggly for a minute when they show up with me, but I won't care at that point." Vance didn't think this was going to be possible before today. Yes, he'd get his men, but he didn't think he'd be coming home again. But with this help, magical help, he thought for sure that he might just make it out without prison time.

Things were set in motion. And when he left to go home,

leaving the little trackers with his brother, he had the ones in his pocket that Raven had made for him. He would only have two weeks to get in, get the job finished, and get out. Not nearly as much time as he thought he might need, but he stood a better chance at it now that he could literally be in two places at once.

Poe was on his porch when he got home. Letting the big raven in was becoming a nightly thing for him. As soon as the two of them were settled in his bedroom, Poe began pacing while he cleaned his guns. He'd get to it soon enough. Vance had learned that rushing him wouldn't get him any closer to talking than just letting him speak his mind.

"You will be in trouble once you leave here." He said that he was aware of that. "I should like to send someone with you. Someone that I can trust."

"I don't need anyone else getting hurt over this, Poe. While I do appreciate you thinking of it, I just—"

"It's not a human, but a fae. Small enough that no one would notice. And when you have done what you need, she can help you more than anyone will be able to in getting out." He asked him if this was a ploy to get him to his mate. "Nay, my lord. I know where she is, as does Raven. She isn't here."

He thought about asking what she was, but knew that he'd not tell him. There was a great deal riding on this, and if he knew he would be afraid that someone else would. Asking the bird what this fae would do for him, Vance sat on his bed.

"She is magical, of course, and old. Very old. And her magic is white, so she will only be true to you once she has become a part of you." Vance asked how that happens. "Much like the sword that you wear upon your back. She will...her name is

Lilac. When she is a part of you, no one will think her anything but a tattoo that you've gotten. But she can hide herself on you, move along your skin so that no one will be the wiser should you not want them to see her."

"Will I know when she moves?" Poe said that he'd need to. "All right. Will she be safe being on my body? As I said, I want no one hurt in this that doesn't need to be."

"She will become a part of you." He wasn't sure what he meant at first, then it occurred to him. She'd be just as immortal as he was. "While she is very old, she can die just as anything can that is magical. Not I nor Raven, since we are a part of each other, and since she mated to young Lewis, she took on what he is. And he her. Am I making you understand, Lord Vance?"

"Yes, and don't call me lord, please. So this being, she's all right with becoming a part of me? Helping me out with this?" He said that she was more than pleased to help him. "Bring her here and I'll talk to her, okay? But it'll have to be soon. I want to get going tonight."

"She is here now." The little being flew to land on his leg. "Lilac, this is the gentleman that I told you about. He is agreeable to allow you to help him, but he has questions."

"I am very happy to meet you, Lord Vance." Poe asked her, as Vance had him, not to call him lord. "I'm sorry. What would you wish for me to call you? I can call you whatever you wish."

"Vance is fine. You don't mind helping me? I don't want you to feel obligated to this. I can do this on my own, but with help, any help, I might make it out in one piece." She glanced at Poe, then smiled at him. "Are you being made to help me?"

"Oh no. I have won the plea to help you. Poe is very special to our kind, and he asked for someone to go with you to help bring you home so that the dragons could be here again. I am very pleased to be the one that was picked. You will be happy with me as well." Vance laughed. "You think me funny?"

"No. I think it's funny that someone wants to help me. I thought I'd have to do this on my own, and now I find that I don't think I could have, and everyone is being very kind to me. I'm not used to it." He asked her what he was to do now. "I mean, you have to be a part of me, how does that work?"

"You only need to roll up your sleeve and I will become a part. You won't be harmed, but you will know that I'm here. And I can do anything you wish." He asked her like what. "I can see things for you. Leave your body long enough that I can find where you need to go. Heal you, should you need it. Also, I can be used as a weapon, but only for a short time as it drains me."

The knock at the door made him stand, and before he could guess what was going on, Lilac left and returned in seconds. He didn't ask her who it was when she put her fingers to her lips, but nodded to his sleeve. Rolling it up, she became a part of him.

Go out the window and I'll help you. The man at the door wishes to come in and put in devices to watch you. I have told Poe, and he will warn the others. He thanked her. *No need, my...Vance, we'll work together.*

Going out the window was the strangest thing he'd ever had happen to him. He didn't jump, as he thought he'd have to, but floated down to the ground with a soft thud. Vance and his fae were across the yard and into the woods in moments. This might work, he thought as he ran to his vehicle.

Chapter 13

Micky watched the laptop, though there wasn't anything really going on that she needed to watch; everything she had running was in the background. But the man that was sitting next to her in the booth was driving her nuts. He kept looking over her shoulder at her screen. Finally, she pulled the earplugs from her ears and asked him what he was doing.

"The Internet is running really slow. Even for this place. I was wondering if you were having the same issues." She told him she was reading a book. "Oh, so you'd not know if it was running slow or not."

"No. I don't care." Putting the plugs back in her ears, she shut him out. There was nothing coming through the plugs, just a thing that usually deterred anyone from talking to her. But this guy was insistent, and when he sat down across from her at her table, she pulled her gun from out of her waistband and aimed at him under the table. "I didn't invite you to sit with me."

"I know. I was wanting to get to know you. You know, sort of talk." She told him no and to go away. "You're not terribly friendly, are you?"

"No. I'm positively bitchy. Now, I'm not going to ask you again to go away. I have shit I'm doing here, and you're bothering me." He sipped whatever it was he was drinking and didn't move. She was going to have to get rid of this piece of shit before she had to pack up and go. "Why aren't you moving?"

"I know what you're doing." She didn't even blink at him. "You're using up the data here by doing something covert."

"And you figured this out how?" He winked at her and she rolled her eyes. "You really think you're smart, don't you? I'm reading a book. I'm here because I like the quietness of the place, and the fact that you can get a good meal and endless drinks while you're at it. I'm not going to tell you again to get away."

The plug in her ear signaled that she was finished uploading the information. The man in front of her didn't move, so she laid her gun on her lap and started packing her shit up. He put his hand on hers when she closed her computer.

"You don't want to do that." Cocking a brow at him, she said nothing. "You have to wait right here until I get the signal that you can go. Which, I'm thinking, you're not going anywhere but with us."

This shit was getting real. Not that she was afraid, but she didn't want anyone else to get hurt either. Picking up her computer, she was careful not to let her gun fall. After putting the computer away and wrapping up her cords, she stuffed it all in her bag. Putting her hands in her lap, she wrapped her hand around the gun and waited on him to make a move.

He reached into his coat, and she saw the butt of the gun before he cleared his coat. Firing twice at him, she could see the shock on his face as the bullets entered his gut. Waiting just long enough for him to slump forward, she took her things and left the place. Pulling out her phone, she pushed a single number and said nothing as the person on the other end answered.

Breaking the phone in half, she put it on the ground outside the restaurant and used a bit of magic to destroy it. Not just the phone, but everything about it...SIM card, battery, and anything else that someone might be able to use. She was to her bike when she snapped her fingers, and all manner of camera and recording devices within a six-mile radius were destroyed.

Micky had about two minutes before the man was discovered. There would be police involved, no doubt, but they'd have no leads to go on. Not from her, anyway. As soon as she started up her bike, she was on the move when the first cruiser passed her. Stopping at a phone booth, which was getting harder and harder to find, she called in to her friend.

"You get it?" He said that he had, all of it. Then he mentioned that the police were on the way to the place she'd been. "Yeah, I think he made me, but it matters little. There is no one that can identify me."

Her hair changed along with her appearance while she stood there. Her clothing was now a pair of jeans and a sweat shirt; the skirt and blouse were gone. She had on boots and not heels, and her hair was no longer blonde but brown. That was the only thing that wasn't her normal self.

"This is what we've been looking for. How did you get it so fast?" Jeff didn't ask because he wanted to out her, but was excited that she'd been able to get it at all. "I'll get this to my contact now. He can use it. By the way, you said that you'd come here for a few days. I'm holding you to that."

"I'm working right now on something else, but I'll come to you soon." He said that wasn't good enough. "Has to be. I have to get my shit together here before someone comes hunting for me again. This time I won't be so nice and instead will beat him for information that I need."

"You be careful."

Looking at the timer on her watch, she ended the call. There wasn't anyone that she trusted more than Jeff, but she also didn't want to leave herself open for anyone to track the two of them down. Going back to her bike, she put it in the back of the stashed van and made her way across town, fucking with her image and vehicle every mile or so. Cameras were everywhere, and she wasn't going to get caught up in that kind of mess.

Two hours after the news started in on how a man had been murdered at a local dive, she was packing up her things again. Not that she ever had that much laying around, and nothing that wasn't replaceable, but she had to be on the move, and the sooner the better.

Micky Oliver had been working computers since someone had thrown one out in their trash and she'd found it. Fixing it had been easy enough, and enhancing it had been even easier. Once she figured out all the things that she could manipulate it to do, she started making a name for herself as a hacker.

Hank Hacker was well known in the underworld. Not by

her own doing, but by Jeff. He said that she needed to have a following, as he did, because when the shit was about to hit the fan, they'd be the ones to warn them. Without the help of the other hackers she had known, Micky would have been caught a few times.

Micky drove all night, and when she reached the outskirts of the little town that Jeff lived in, just to make sure he was all right, she pulled into a hotel that had outside doors and took one of the rooms. She was settling in when she realized she was hungry. This wasn't normal for her unless she was using a little too much of her magic, so she found a restaurant that had a salad bar and made her way there, changing herself again to appear to be an elderly woman.

Fresh was what she needed, and as soon as she was brought her first glass of juice, she drained it while looking around. There was a family in one corner trying to feed three teenagers that were being asses. A couple of truckers that were in need of not just a bath, but maybe some disinfectant as well. And the lone waitress. Micky pulled out her cell, also enhanced, and called Jeff again.

"Got it all?" He said that he did and had already sent it to his friend. "Look, I might have to lay low for a couple of days. I'm not myself."

He, like anyone else who thought they knew her, didn't have a clue what she was or what she was capable of. Jeff was good at what he did, but she was better. And stronger when she was up to par. Which, she wasn't right now.

"All right. I wish you'd come stay here. That way I could keep an eye on you while you rested up." She thanked him and told him for now she was fine. "I'll talk to you in a few days, all right?"

"Yes, all right." She put the phone away and watched the two newcomers. One was obviously a cop, the other she'd bet was military. They never looked her way, but she still thought they were there for her. When she made another trip to the bar, she made sure that she got as much fruit and other fresh things as she could on her plate before going by their table. The moment they looked up at her, she knew she was in trouble.

Knowing that she could leave right now and they'd not be able to follow, she needed information more than she did running right now. The men knew something, but getting it from them would be tricky. Lifting up her gun, she shot the first one in the back, the military guy, and then she killed the cop when he stood up. In a matter of seconds she was out the door with macho man.

He would live, she knew that, but when he shot her three times while she was carrying him, she nearly dropped him as she flew over the hillside. The pain was too much, so when she was far enough away, she let him drop to the ground as she landed beside him.

"Fucker, that wasn't nice." Taking his gun and any other weapon he had on him, she put them in her pockets. Time to get what she needed. And since she was hurting like a mother fucker, she decided to do things her way.

Letting herself go, she felt her wings spread out behind her. It felt glorious after being so confined for so long. Using them to fly didn't give her the feeling like she had with just stretching them. She smiled at the man when he cringed away from her.

"They didn't tell you what I was?" He said nothing. "Oh, well, that won't work for me. I need for you to talk. If not, I'll have to get it from you the hard way. What's it going to be? Talking or the raping of your small mind?"

"They don't know what you are. Said a woman, that's all." Micky waited for him to continue. "What the fuck gave us away? I was told that you were not all that smart when cornered."

"Too bad you're not going to get to go back and warn them. Who sent you?" Nothing. "Seriously? I'm bleeding here, and you can't tell me shit? Who sent you?"

She didn't have time to wait around for him to get his shit together and tell her. Putting her hand on his head, she ignored his screams of pain as she sorted through his mind. There was plenty to see too, if someone knew how to look. Once she got all that she could, Micky stood up and paced. The man was dead now — she'd not been nice about her search — but she had information that was going to hurt a few dozen people if she didn't get it to someone fast.

"What to do? What to do?" She had to clear her mind and find someplace to heal. She could, but without something to eat that was high in sugar, and fresh, she'd be months and not days healing. She'd not die, but she couldn't heal herself without consequences.

When the cell phone at his side started chirping, she picked it up and saw that the name on it was unknown. Whoever it was on the other end, they might not know that he was dead. Or they might, and were trying to pinpoint her by her answering. So she was back to her first question. What to do?

Answering it, she said nothing but watched the time. "My

name is Caelin. You don't know me, but I have a safe haven for you, Micky. But I don't imagine that you'd trust me any more than you do anyone else. All right. Let me come to you."

Before she could tell him that was a bad idea, a man was standing in front of her. Pulling her gun out, she aimed it right at his chest when he laughed. There wasn't shit about this that was funny as far as she was concerned.

"It will do you no good to shoot me. I mean, it will hurt, yes, but I won't die. Neither will you." Micky could smell his magic...it was as white as the driven snow. "Here you go. I know that you can tell if something is tainted. Go ahead and feast on this while I talk."

The oranges and apples were beautiful. Shiny, like he'd rubbed them against something soft before putting them on the plate. Sitting down on the ground, she didn't waver her gun when he sat as well. The food helped a great deal, and she moaned when a gallon of fresh pear juice was set beside her.

"What are you?" He told her. "Dragon? They're all dead. Or in hiding. And I know better than most that the shifter dragons have all been in hiding for a very long time."

"Yes, they have been, I'm afraid." She ate another apple while he continued. "They're in Ohio, these shifters. I had thought you'd make it there on your own, but there is something searching for you that I hadn't counted on. You're not as well hidden as I had thought."

"No shit, Sherlock. The president, of all people, is after my ass. Who would have thought it?" He said that he hadn't. "So, you're a dragon and you knew that I was here. Want to explain that to me?"

"Not at the moment, no. Besides, I think you'd be better served if I told you what you needed to do now, and the rest will come to you." She nodded and leaned back to watch him. "You're not trusting, not that I blame you, but you must trust me for a time."

"Why should I? I mean, yes, the fruit you brought was good, and needed. You did find me. And used a phone that might not have been easily tapped. So what gives?" He handed her a piece of paper, and she only glanced at it before shrugging. "Who hasn't heard of the jewels that bring the dragons back? Most people with money have been looking for them all my life."

"Yes, but what most don't know is that they're all coming together soon. Very soon, as a matter of fact. But you need to help one of them before he can return to his home." She asked him why she'd do that. "Because you need your dragon to come to life again."

She said nothing to him, but did look at her thigh. The dragon there, a sigil, most people thought, was her very own bit of magic. He'd gone to sleep the day that the queen of the castle that she'd lived in had disappeared.

"She's my mother, Queen Prisane, she's my mother. And she lives." Shaking her head, she stared at the man, who was nodding. "You heard about me, I'm sure. The child of the bastard Butler, who was going to make things right. And how I had to live to make the dragons come back."

"As I said before, everyone has heard of that tale. And that's all it is, a tale." When he stood up, she did as well. His shift from man to dragon made her eyes fill with tears. To see something so magnificent was heartwarming. The magic that he brought with him, it not only healed her, but gave her more energy as well. "You're really him? And Warrior, where is he?"

"He is waiting for them to come together this final time." Micky wasn't sure she wanted to believe him or not, but he was making a good case for himself. "I need for you to go and help one of the men. He will not return when I need for him to, and all will be lost."

"He's one of the dragons. The family that is supposed to be able to call him forth." Caelin nodded. "Why me? I'm nothing but a faerie gone rogue. Even my own kind won't have a thing to do with me. They think me tainted in the head."

"I would say that they're right on that, a little anyway. Someone that has taught herself how to use what most of them shun and make it work for her. You must have a couple of things in that head of yours that is different than them." She grinned at him, and he laughed. "Will you help me with this? I can guarantee you that you will be greatly rewarded when this is done."

"I don't want a reward." Micky wondered if he'd do her a favor, and when he said he'd do anything for her, she sat there for several seconds thinking. Trust, as he pointed out, wasn't something that she had a great deal of. "I don't need the money, but the pip that I came from, they could use some help. I send them what I can, in way of a messenger, but they need more."

"I can make sure that they not only have gardens to work in, but that they are cared for as well." Micky's parents lived in a glen that was being overrun by development. It was killing them, but no matter how many times she'd gone there to

202

help them move on, she'd been ignored. No, not ignored, but shunned. "I will not tell them who is helping them until the time is right."

"They won't go if you tell them." Caelin nodded. "All right. I don't know why I'm trusting you, but I am. You do this for me, and I'll agree to help this man for you."

Taking his hand when offered, she felt the surge of more magic fill her and the feeling of moving. When she opened her eyes, she was alone in a dark room. There were things going on behind the door to her left, but she stood still. She had no idea what she was in here for.

"He will come to you in a moment or two. Do not try and kill him. His name is Vance. He's not trusting either, but you will need to listen to him. For if you don't, all will be lost." She asked him if he was going to get them killed. "No. He is, like you, an immortal."

~~~

Vance opened the door to the little room and stood there until the men who were walking the halls moved on. Before he could make good on his escape, he felt the presence of something behind him. Turning with his gun drawn, he saw her shining in the corner. The small wave she gave him had him cursing under his breath.

"Yeah, I know just how you feel. I'm Micky, by the way. I was sent here by Caelin to help get your ass out of this jam. Whatever the fuck you're into, anyway. And where are we?" Vance didn't need this. But he was in a little bit of a jam. "Are you stupid? Or just ignoring me?"

"Neither. I'm trying to figure out if I need to kill you or

use you." He looked her up and down and felt his cock stretch. "Both sound good right now."

She had a knife at his throat before he moved. At least he thought it was a knife. The wings behind her explained the sparkling shit, but not what she was doing here. He put his finger on the blade to move it and felt it prick his skin. This wasn't going to end well for him if she hurt him more.

"I'm here to help you. I was told that you'd have to explain things so that I could." He said that he needed to get out of there before they were caught in order to make that happen. "Why didn't you say so?"

He didn't know where they were, but he could see the ocean right outside the window he was by. Not only was there a great view of it, but he could see ships in the distance and knew they were shrimping. Looking around the place, he knew that they were in a hotel, but not how they'd gotten there. Micky was sitting on the couch eating an apple. When she tossed him one, he caught it and sat down across from her. Things were too weird for him to compile any questions for the moment. So he ate the apple.

"I'm a faerie. Rogue, if you need to know that. But I have a lot of magic that can help you should you be okay with that. And for the record, I don't usually ask, but Caelin is doing me a favor, and I told him I'd help. What were we doing in the White House, and why was the Secret Service told to look for you and shoot you on sight?" Vance said he wasn't aware they knew he was there. "Yes. That guy of yours, I think his name was Sam... no, sorry, Samuel, he gave you up two days ago. Want another apple?"

"He'd not do that." She nodded and tossed him an apple. "How do you know that? I mean, last time I saw him, he was at the hotel where we were staying."

"They got to him. And he didn't give you up easily. They did things to him that I've not seen used on humans before. Peeled his skin off in the most delicate of places. But he didn't tell them everything, only that you were coming for them. The president is looking for me too, but for a different reason." Vance nodded. "We have a mutual friend too. Jeff Burner. He goes by Prick Stick. I just sent him a lot of information. Information that apparently is coming, or has gotten, to you."

"No, nothing yet. But then I'm not at my hiding place." She moved to the computer that he wasn't sure was there before, and when she sat down, he stood behind her. When she brought it all up and moved out of the chair, he sat down. "This is what I needed. You got it?"

"Yes. I'm better at getting in and out of computers than he is sometimes." She was eating again, more fruit. He asked her what she'd meant by being rogue. "My family has disowned me. Mostly because of what I do...kill when I need to, and I have, a lot. Also, I'm not very nice. Ever."

"Yeah, right there with you on that one." He read over a few more pages, and asked her when she'd gotten this. She told him earlier that morning. "This has information on Samuel, and that he's being taken in for questioning."

"He's dead, as I said. They did things to him that wouldn't have let him last long." Standing up, he asked her if she was leaving. "No. I thought I'd take a dip in the water here. I don't get places like this often. If you need me, just yell. Or join me.

There is shit you can put on in the bedroom on your left. Mine is back here."

When he finished the report, she was on the beach that was perhaps ten yards from the door he was looking out of. Her hair was wet, and he could see that instead of being red, like he knew it to be, it was darker because of the water. Thinking about Caelin and the reasons for sending her here, he wasn't really surprised when he appeared beside him.

"She's your mate. I had to send her to you so that you two could work this out." Vance said he'd figured that out the moment he'd found himself in the closet with her. "I thought you might. But she can help you. And she can be trusted. I don't know how long it will take for either of you to get to that point on your own, but she's there for you to work with."

"What's with the fruit? I understand that she's a faerie, but they don't have to eat all the time." He said that she'd been shot that morning. "And do I want to know by who?"

"The president is after her. He's found out about her abilities, none of them to do with her computer skills. He wishes to use her as a weapon." Vance looked down at his own weapon. "Lilac can help you both now. But you should know that Micky is much stronger."

"Sending her here with me, isn't that breaking the rules? I mean, what if we're both caught up in this? Then what?" Caelin said nothing. "She's the key, isn't she? The one that not only saves us all, but me in the process. What if I don't want to be saved? Have you thought of that?"

"I have, and you do need to be saved." Vance snorted. "Yes, she can do that as well as you. But without you two coming together, I mean in a working relationship, this will end badly for a great many people. And the man that she killed…well, she raped his mind and found out about you too. They're searching for the two of you, but for different reasons."

"She said that." Caelin nodded but didn't say what her reasons were. Abilities could mean just about anything. "You said she was strong. What are her abilities, other than she can move through space and time in a second?"

"Watch her."

They did, both of them, when she stood up, after blowing a kiss his way, she morphed into herself again…a faerie with red wings and red sparks. While Vance watched her, she raised her arms above her head and he staggered back. The blades that appeared on every part of her flesh had him mesmerized. Then the blades shot toward them both, hitting everything around them without once touching either of them.

Turning around, he saw a perfect outline of the two of them, but he and Caelin hadn't been touched by the thousands of shards that he could see now were glass, not blades. Vance looked at her again when she said his name.

"Come join me. The water is fantastic. Then when we've enjoyed it for a little while, we'll go take care of the monsters in the White House."

Vance looked at Caelin, but he was gone. In his place was a basket of fruit, as well as a note. Picking it up, he read the words there before bursting out in laughter.

Tread carefully.

Kathi Barton, winner of the Pinnacle Book Achievement award as well as a best-selling author on Amazon and All Romance books, lives in Nashport, Ohio with her husband Paul. When not creating new worlds and romance, Kathi and her husband enjoy camping and going to auctions. She can also be seen at county fairs with her husband who is an artist and potter.

Her muse, a cross between Jimmy Stewart and Hugh Jackman, brings her stories to life for her readers in a way that has them coming back time and again for more. Her favorite genre is paranormal romance with a great deal of spice. You can visit Kathi online and drop her an email if you'd like. She loves hearing from her fans. aaronskiss@gmail.com.

Follow Kathi on her blog: http://kathisbartonauthor.blogspot.com/

www.ingramcontent.com/pod-product-compliance
Lightning Source LLC
Chambersburg PA
CBHW031956170626
46807CB00006B/2513